PAPA'S SUITCASE

PAPA'S SUITCASE

a novel by

Gerhard Köpf

translated by A. Leslie Willson

GEORGE BRAZILLER   NEW YORK

First published in the United States of America in 1995 by
George Braziller, Inc.

English translation copyright © 1994 by A. Leslie Willson
Originally published in German

Copyright © 1994 by Luchterhand Literaturverlag,
Hamburg under the title *Papas Koffer*

For information, write to the publisher:

George Braziller, Inc.
60 Madison Avenue
New York, NY 10010

ISBN 0-8076-1342-8

A catalog record of this book is available at the Library of
Congress

Printed in the United States

What you are depends upon what you've read by chance.

—Elias Canneti

1

My big fish must be somewhere. Admittedly, I haven't found it yet, but I'm not giving up. There are many reasons to be on the move. Some people are always running away from something; others, like me, are always searching. But I know for certain that the empty space of expectation never matches the shape of fulfillment. Recognizing that, what are we to do, if not travel in pursuit of our wishes?

The land here is beautiful, but probably you would be more likely to find a McDonald's in Timbuktu than in the cemetery of Ketchum, Idaho. After confusingly endless roads, crisscross information, missed connections, and time-consuming detours I finally arrived at my destination. And between two pines at the foot of the Sawtooth Mountains I found the grave for which I had so long searched. It lay next to that of Taylor Williams, an old hunting friend who had passed on two years earlier.

The view from the fifty-thousand-dollar concrete structure, clad in wood after the American custom—in which at about seven-thirty on the morning of July 2, 1961, Papa shot off the top of his skull with a double-barreled Richardson, and in doing so cast doubt upon everything that he had previously stood for—was breathtaking. To the north and the south I could see the tent-like mountains of the region, and through the wide windows eastward the winding course of the Big Wood River, its banks lined with aspens and poplars. At the other end of the board, flat valley I visualized the grass-green stripe of the cemetery.

While I was staring out the window I remembered the statement by Dr. George Savers, Sun Valley: "I didn't notice that he was nearing his end until once I was sitting with him in the vestibule and, weeping, he said: 'Nothing more is coming. It doesn't work anymore, George.' He could no longer write. I noticed especially the thinness of his legs and arms. His face was pale and shot with red veins. He only groped his way forward. My strongest impression was of his fragility. He spoke with isolated scraps of words, hardly ever in sentences. He was a total wreck and looked years older than he was: white-haired, trembling, obviously very sick, distressed, and sad. That was shortly before he went to the Mayo Clinic and got those terrible electric shock treatments. Nothing worse could have happened to him."

Meanwhile I am familiar with the weary lines moving forward in the waiting rooms all over the world: gray married couples in silent struggle; young parents packed with bottles, diapers, and senseless toys for squabbling children; backpack people with crusts of dirt between their toes. And no sight is better suited to dissuade someone from traveling than the departure lounge of a large airport.

When you travel a lot and most of the time are alone on trains, in planes, and in strange hotels, you get the oddest thoughts at times because you're out of touch. You think you would like to have all the time in the world, but when you do get it, it's an illusion. There are questions to which you return again and again at certain moments. Reflect on them however long you want, the old problem comes up anew: How could everything turn out to be the way it is now? One way or another you then try to find the beginning, but wherever you begin: There's always the same result.

You're really happy only when you don't think about it.

2

nd yet I know exactly how it began with me. Actually, I wanted to become something very different, and in doing so be a totally different person than I am now. But I bet there's hardly anyone who ever became what he once originally planned. And then at a bar somewhere or in a waiting room you meet a stranger with whom, little by little, you get into a conversation. One word leads to another, you ask about whence and whither, and already you're netted by your own memories and start talking about yourself to a total stranger who's not concerned with all that or not at all interested in it. But that doesn't bother you, because you'd just like to talk to someone.

10

In my case everything began in that unending, long, hot summer in which I left school. The trees were higher, the fields wider, the paths longer, the valley greener. Somehow that summer changed my life. And possibly the story begins with the fact that I wanted to become a stonecutter and make grave monuments, a real stonemason who sets tombstones and inscribes them or carves mourning angels who look up to Heaven, or God knows where, with drooping wings, holding a funeral wreath in their hands. Yes, that's exactly the kind of person I wanted to become. Earlier I wanted to become a roustabout at the annual fair, helping put up the Ferris wheel and the shooting gallery, pounding the stakes into the ground for the big tent, and get all kinds of free rides on the carousel. But now it was time for a grave monument stonecutter.

"But always just at the cemetery and among the dead?" my grandmother expressed her misgivings about whether that was the right thing for someone my age.

I wasn't exactly sure, I just knew that I wanted to drop out of school after the tenth grade. Not that I had gotten bad grades—about average, I would say—but I just had had enough and wanted finally to start doing something with my hands and with my fancied strength. Because as a child I always had my pants pockets full of stones, I decided on training in stonemasonry. I believed firmly that I would learn a lot about stones and be able to do something with them that pleased other people as well.

My grandmother, who raised me because my parents had lost their lives in a traffic accident when I was still very small, wasn't exactly enthusiastic about my plan but in the end, after she had again laid out her cards as she did before all important decisions, had nothing against it and, even though shaking her head, agreed. That was many years ago, but at certain moments, when the old images return, it seems to me as though it were only yesterday.

3

People in Pamplona whom I asked about Papa, and who had nothing else in their heads but bulls and priests, knew nothing about a suitcase, rather only about a flabby, insufferable old man, sitting around indolently, plagued by hepatitis, diabetes, high blood pressure, skin cancer, arteriosclerosis, and alcoholism: "As soon as he had gone to his room, he had begun a sentence and written it completely, but afterward he could not go on writing. He drew a line through it, started a second sentence, and then was again confronted with total emptiness. He was incapable of writing the next sentence, although he knew what it was. He again wrote a first, simple, declarative sentence, and again it was impossible for him to get the next sentence down on paper. He could write no more than one sentence, and the sentences kept getting more simpleminded and were completely asinine."

But I was thinking of something else. I held monologues and said: *To me Heaven would be a big bullring with me holding two barrera seats and a trout stream outside that no one else was allowed to fish in and two lovely houses in the town: one where I would have my wife and children . . . and the other where I would have my nine beautiful mistresses on nine different floors. . . . Then there would be a fine church like in Pamplona where I could go to confession on the way from one house to the other, and I would get on my horse and ride out with my son to my bull ranch named Hacienda Hadley and toss coins to all my illegitimate children that lived [along] the road. I would write out at the hacienda and send my son in to lock chastity belts onto my mistresses because someone had just galloped up with the news that a notorious monogamist named Fitzgerald had been seen riding toward the town at the head of a company of strolling drinkers.*

4

In reality everything began naturally when I started to read the short stories of Hemingway, who was still alive at the time. It was like an infection with a lifelong high fever. Perhaps at the time I already had the wish, without knowing it, of one day no longer finding things out of books but of dissolving totally in them and disappearing in them. My fodder for reading—I have to put it that way because it was really like nourishment to me—I obtained from an old bookseller named Lemming, who sold mainly souvenirs, school notebooks, and pen cases, as well as maps of the nearby surroundings, and for a long time was said to have lived in India. At least that's what people who found him weird told one another. When one day he campaigned for the preservation of the waterwheel of the old foundry and walked around Thulsern with a collection box, people disparagingly called him the Waterwheel Professor. I, on the other hand, visited him gladly, listened to his stories about stoical elephants and English officers, about Hindu boys and fairy-tale maharanis, stories that often enough consisted only of incomprehensible hints or suffocated in a curious giggle, and I'm still grateful to him today for the suggestions for reading that he gave me. I could always depend upon him.

He always said then: "I have something for you again that you will like. I can only put out the apples for you. You have to eat them yourself. But read carefully and then let me know. I want to know precisely. And if you don't like a book sometime, then you can exchange it. I don't want it lying around your place unread and not be available for someone else who would perhaps like it. And don't forget: It's not a matter of what was, but of what could have been. When you read, it's only a matter of possibilities. Never forget that! Books offer you nothing more than possibilities. Books show you the blue path. The blue path is the path of the possible. You have to find out what nests between the lines. It's a matter of the inner lining, do you understand? That's like with a potato. You don't eat the stalk, but the tuber, and that's under the dirt. You don't see it."

He really did demand detailed information and wouldn't be put off with superficial impressions. He bored deeper. But it was nonetheless not like in school. It was somehow different, more intensive. It always had to do with books, not with the essay that was supposed to be written about them. With his interrogations, he taught me how to read precisely. Little by little that pedantically exact Waterwheel Professor enveloped me with what had appeared by Hemingway in paperback. Back then the wretchedly bound paperbacks, with awful paper, were a bargain for the little money I earned on the side at all kinds of jobs. I made a bookcase for them from a simple board and put it up over my bed. My first bookcase. I carefully polished it with an emery cloth, rounded off the corners, and painted it black. It really looked good. There stood my Hemingway. Today those tattered volumes are the jewels of my library, and I still often take a volume down, put it carefully in my luggage, and then remember less the contents of the book than the mood in which I read it for the first time. On the last page of the book under the ending I always wrote the date on which I had finished a book. That way a mysterious calendar came into being that lived its own life next to the real calendar and made it easy for me to retrieve periods of reading long past.

It was a fairly hot summer, and on graduation day I lay down in the afternoon behind a shady haystack. All I needed at that moment was something new, because our godforsaken place was so desolate that the sparrows flew backward from boredom. I felt as if, on a bright morning after a long winter, I were turning a new page, and I read and read. While doing so, I chewed on a licorice stick that we called a bear turd back then. I will never forget the bitter taste on my tongue. I will always associate it with reading. And it seemed to me that the birches over on the moor suddenly were gleaming whiter:

Why did he kill himself, Daddy?

I don't know. . . . He couldn't stand things, I guess.

Do many men kill themselves, Daddy?

Not very many. . . .

Do many women?

Hardly ever.

Don't they ever?

Oh, yes. They do sometimes.

Daddy?

Yes. . . .

Is dying hard, Daddy?

No, I think it's pretty easy. It all depends.

They were seated in the boat, [the boy] in the stern, his father rowing. The sun was coming up over the hills. A bass jumped, making a circle in the water. [The boy] trailed his hand in the water. It felt warm in the sharp chill of the morning.

In the early morning on the lake, sitting in the stern of the boat with his father rowing, he felt quite sure that he would never die.

My favorite passage: First the short dialogue about death, then the boy in the stern of the boat, the rowing father, whom I see before me as well as the leaping bass, the hand in the water in the sharp morning chill.

And in addition the boy's certainty of never dying.

Of course, I immediately imagined sitting with my own father in such a boat, but I didn't have a father, and hardly a memory of him. Perhaps that's why this passage made such an impression on me.

5

That was really always my favorite passage, and even today I know the lines by heart. How often had I read them? Now I know: You always read the right book at the right time.

For me, reading meant landing a fish. To me it explained the world and my place in it; black on white, it let me participate in something that, I knew, involved me personally in a mysterious way. In books I accommodated the life that I myself would like to have lived. I loved stories that told the losers about the end of the victors. I found strange memoirs more exciting than my own. The biographies of people who had published their life as their work fascinated me especially. And in Hemingway I read:

All good books have one thing in common: They are truer than if they had really happened, and after you've read one, you will feel that all that happened, happened to you and then it belongs to you forever: the happiness and unhappiness, the good and evil, ecstasy and sorrow, the food, wine, beds, people, and the weather. If you can give that to readers, then you're a writer.

No, it was not a matter of finding myself, as they say today, for after all my experiences I am now convinced that so-called finding yourself is psychological nonsense. For me it was a matter of the unending, enduring process of reading. I see the uncoupling of mind from emotions as a chief malady of my age.

I had the best and most valuable experiences while reading because I expanded my imagination that way. For me, reading was a conversation with myself. A search of my conscience, confession and absolution in one.

I not only incorporated Hemingway's stories into myself. I wanted to transform myself into them. His words became my words. Reading him was beautiful. And never again have I read the way I did that long, hot summer. Never again was I so drunk on letters of the alphabet, never again did my ears and brow glow so, never again has my heart

21

beat so wildly, never again have I taken such images with me into sleep. Books were bequests into which I could creep. They transformed my Thulsern into the area of upper Michigan. And books not only administered ancient wisdom, they became it and stood at the ready. Only for me.

6

B ut soon on that afternoon, the letters began to dance before my eyes. I merely skimmed the lines, leafed aimlessly here and there, I smelled the book a bit and then my hands, as though that could substitute for reading, I laid the paperback next to me and closed my eyes, and saw myself bustling about, covered with dust, wearing a huge apron, in the workshop of the stonecutter. It cost me some effort to find my way back to Hemingway's short stories, and even then I suspected that on that afternoon I would manage at the most a few more lines. That didn't bother me further because I had the feeling that the times were now gone in which, as at school, I needed to do nothing more than exert my brain. For that reason I observed my hands attentively, felt my muscles, found them sturdy enough for living, but noticed with disappointment that my fingers were fairly slender and too smooth really to grab hold of something. But that would change abruptly when I was working with a hammer and chisel and got the first splits in my skin, of which I would be as proud as an Indian would. I was looking forward to that and could hardly wait for it.

At this time especially I began to miss my parents. Not that I had felt ill at ease with Grandmother, but somehow I longed for a father and a mother and a real family. My parents had died in a bus accident, and I had practically no memory of them, for I was exactly two years old at the time. They had traveled into the lowlands, and in a thick snowfall the bus had run off the road and plunged down an embankment. Some were injured, some seriously injured, and two were dead.

Only much, much later did this story turn out to be a pious fabrication by my grandmother. Through stupid chance I discovered that my parents had committed suicide. My father suffered from a congenital melancholy from which he knew no way out. Life was more and more tedious for him and at last became unbearable. He first shot my mother and then himself.

What remained of my parents lay in a shoe box: a few
photographs, a wallet, and my mother's bridal bouquet.
More and more frequently I looked at the photos and tried to
find out what kind of people they might have been. My
grandmother, my father's mother, seldom and unwillingly
spoke about them because usually tears welled in her eyes.
But she always emphasized how wonderful they both had
been and how much they had loved me. They had also been
very much in love with one another, and she couldn't understand, even today, just why these two had had to die. My
father had been in the war, and soon after his return from
captivity I had come into the world. The more I looked at
the photos, the more I noticed that I was comparing my
father to Hemingway. There were a number of similarities:
the beard, the broad head, and the immense shoulders, the
big jacket, and how he stood firmly on the ground with both
legs. My mother must have been rather delicate. She was
considerably shorter than Father and had hair cut short. In
one photograph these strange people were laughing happily
at one another. It had been taken shortly after my birth. My
mother was already over forty when she had me. My father
was two years younger. They went to Meran on their honey-
moon. My father had large hands for an elementary school
teacher, almost as large as those of Hemingway in the pic-

ture where he's holding the cat in his arms. Grandmother had put the photographs into a shoe box and kept on planning to paste them in an album.

"I'm definitely still going to do that. But I just don't get around to it. The right moment will still come along," she said.

"That's all right," I said, because I liked rummaging in the shoe box more than leafing carefully through an album.

"It'd have to be an album with tissue paper between the pages. So that the pictures are well protected," said Grandmother, "and under every picture I'd have to write the date. But I have such a hard time remembering. I think I'm already too old. I've forgotten a great deal already."

"An album like that is expensive," I tried to console her.

"I don't know either whether it'd really be worth it."

"There's a nice jumble in the box. I like that," I said.

"You are and will remain a numbskull," she said. And I thought of Hemingway and my father's broad shoulders. I could easily imagine him as a bullfighter and big-game hunter. Once I even asked my grandmother whether my father had not written something, whether any letters were preserved or diaries or something like that. But there was nothing of the sort. Maybe Grandmother had simply let those things disappear.

I would like to have asked my father about the war and how it had been earlier. And I wanted to talk to him about fishing and girls and about politics. At the time, Parliament had just decided that the statute of limitations on Nazi murders would not begin for two years. I would have been interested in what Father thought about that, and whether he had shot at anyone during the war. At the time Starfighters were falling out of the sky in droves, but Thulsern was spared. Churchill died, and a hundred million tons of grain was lacking to feed the earth's population. The Mont Blanc Tunnel was opened, an ape's heart had been put into a man, the Emergency Laws were being discussed, and in Frankfurt there was a trial of the Auschwitz criminals. There was mention of that in the readers' circle, as well as about the summer fashions from Paris. They showed an emphatic feminine style: small waists, flaring skirts. All of that I would like to have discussed with my father. I couldn't talk about it to Grandmother. She considered it all stuff and nonsense and just shook her head. She liked much more to bury herself in the horoscope, laid out cards for hours, or mumbled something to herself that I didn't understand. Once she glanced up from her eternal cards, looked at me, and said: "Each one of us has two lives: the one in which he studies, and the other in which he lives after that." But I would like to have rowed with my father across a lake in the early-morning chill.

After the miserable failure of my training as a stonecutter, Grandmother quickly decided to put me into an apprenticeship with my bookseller, and for me began a wonderful time of reading and learning. Unfortunately, the man died quite unexpectedly, and the bookstore had to be dissolved. In the same year my grandmother died, too, and I was alone in the world.

Grandmother had a nice death. One morning she simply didn't wake up. She had become more and more eccentric. At the end she sustained herself only with grilled herring. She didn't want to eat anything else. Sometimes she got the idea that she had to deliver pieces of fretwork: Christmas stars or ponies; sometimes she fell out of bed, became incontinent, gave confused speeches all night long, or with endless patience laid out the cards. But when the King of Hearts came along, she married Caruso and Greta Garbo in the name of the Father, the Son, and the Holy Ghost and asserted that I was an occupation child, sired by a German soldier and a Swede, both of whom had died in a plane crash shortly after my birth. She had adopted me out of pure compassion, but in reality I was a Finn. There was nothing else for me to do but find diapers for Grandmother, tie a bib around her, and into her toothless mouth shove grilled herring, which she soon after threw up. The apartment became noticeably dilapidated, tidying up became more and more wearisome. Grandmother became slovenly. She dropped everything, just wore a ragged, stained housecoat that smelled of urine, and she raised a hue and cry when I wanted to wash it. Sometimes she said not a word for days, then again she couldn't be stopped and talked for hours to herself, said stuff about the past that made no sense, that I didn't know what to make of, mixed up day and night, dream and reality. What she found in the illustrated magazines became reality for her, and she hardly noticed her immediate surroundings.

I, too, shrank to the size of a horoscope. Whatever I did was commented on with a horoscope formula. Typical Virgo, Grandmother said, for example, whenever I cleaned up behind her: conscientious and obstinate to the point of pedantry. I didn't care much about any of that only because I had slipped more and more into Hemingway's skin.

I applied at a university bookstore in the city and was accepted. I spent day after day there for more than a quarter century. Those were hazy years that piled up monotonously in my memory, one after the other. I was bolstered solely by a friend whom I had met one day in the bookstore: Assistant Principal Mürzig. Today I honestly no longer know whether

I really got to know Mürzig or whether I just read about him. But what role does that play for someone for whom the boundaries between what is real and what is read about have become fluid? In short: Mürzig was my only friend and confidant. He had an understanding of my mania for reading; with him I could at least talk sensibly.

7

I belonged to that dying-out breed of booksellers who still read. Books were the only comfort in my unvaried life, full of shades of gray. A day without reading showed me how long eternity could be. When I was reading the classics, I firmly believed that the dead writers were still writing their books. We all live in inaccessible arenas, and if you don't want to be driven up the wall, then you just have to read. Reading is always more sensible than wasting time with some female or other. Of course I read. How could I, as a bookseller, recommend a book that I myself hadn't read? If people were to read more, our world would be better off. That was my motto.

And because I didn't want to give up such views, it stirred up quite a commotion one day.

That afternoon, when the staff meeting had resolved unanimously to reject my Hemingway window display—proposed weeks before and worked out in the smallest detail, with posters, editions, volumes of letters, biographies, selected examples of secondary literature, and facsimiles of handwritten notes—I had left the university bookstore embittered and, though inwardly highly agitated, had complacently strolled in the direction of downtown, as though nothing had happened. In my mind was only one goal: to disappear finally, for disappearance had seemed to me the last possible form of truth.

During the conference all the booksellers had once again made me feel that I belonged on the scrap heap and ostensibly was no longer up-to-date. Meanwhile I had read more than all of them put together. For that reason I liked only customers who at once insisted on all the available books of an author and were not content with this or that new publication.

I knew that everything about me was old except for my eyes. They had the color of the sky and were bright. And again the staff had wanted to force me to take a computer course finally. The time of the fussy rotation of bulky catalogues was over once and for all, they said, only I wasn't willing to understand that because I was imprudent and full of the obstinacy of old age. Beyond that my jealousy about books clearly went too far, when at times I refused to sell them at all. How often had I asserted to a customer whom I found disagreeable that the book was out of print, not obtainable, or had not even appeared. I was particularly disgruntled with customers who asked for a book that had been recommended the evening before by a verbose critic on television. Often enough I had refused to hand over the title requested. Instead, I had merely looked at the customer disdainfully. So-called sniffers, who just opened a book briefly and read here and there at random, I put in their place bluntly: You don't just burst into a restaurant and take this and that arbitrarily from a stranger's plate.

That kind of thing was going decisively too far, my superior had commented, that was behavior that was detrimental to the business. Whereas I had simply just tried to prevent certain books from getting into the wrong hands. After all, you don't sell a Persian rug to a person who's looking for something to spread out in a repair shop. We were talking about casting pearls before swine.

On the other hand, it had been noticed a number of times that in regard to book thieves I had let a comparatively immense leniency prevail; indeed, I had paid for many a stolen book out of my own pocket and let the thief get away scot-free with the remark: Anyone who took such a risk just to swipe a certain book must be an obsessed reader and really need the book urgently. That was not a criminal act: on the contrary!

At one of the unspeakable staff meetings, I had distributed to my coworkers a sheet of paper, described as a *decalogue*, with the following contents:

1) The bookseller is duty bound to regard the buyer as the book's enemy.

2) Books are to be protected as much as possible from the customer.

3) The hours the bookstore is open are to be reduced to an absolute minimum: at maximum a half hour in the very early morning.

4) Free access to the bookshelves is prohibited on principle; the floorwalkers must be armed.

5) Any kind of consultation must fundamentally be denied.

6) The provider of information must be surly, hard-of-hearing, or unavailable.

7) The catalogues must be confusing or illegible.

8) The time between the ordering and delivery of a

book must be unbearably long.

9) A customer may buy a maximum of one book.

10) The books must be sealed in even thicker and more tear-resistant plastics to protect them even better from a (phony) customer.

In addition, I had proposed that future booksellers should be trained like firemen and pass a test in climbing ladders, carrying heavy burdens, et cetera.

My only friend and confidant, Assistant Principal Mürzig, had given me strong moral support in my manifesto. But I had only been smiled at pityingly by the assembled staff.

A fossil, and crazy to boot.

That's how they described me again and again behind my back. And I had felt their glances like arrows and clearly heard their whispering. The atmosphere of the meeting had been poisonous from the beginning. All in all the whole staff of the university bookstore seemed to me like a collection of envious mutton heads and murderous poisoners of wells and had for years been in a state of war: Each hated the other; whenever an opportunity arose a quick coalition formed to put one over on an opponent; but in the final analysis each fought mercilessly against everyone else. I no longer wanted to belong to that kind of destructively quarrelsome bunch. Up until now I had kept out of the trench warfare as long as possible, dutifully but with clearly waning enthusiasm had waited on the mostly ignorant customers, had kept up with my courses in the book-trade school, and had talked in my lectures about the cultural history of reading:

There are some things that cannot be learned quickly, and time, which is all we have, must be paid heavily for their acquiring. They are the very simplest things, and because it takes a man's life to know them, the little new that man gets from life is very costly and the only heritage he has to leave. I have always saved myself in books as though on an island. Books have always intervened in history. Even to the present day they belong to archives and laboratories of our view of the world as well as of our view of ourselves. In them are preserved hopes as well as the contradictions on which hopes are dashed. And even freedom has frequently nested in the beginning and in the end between the letters of the alphabet.

I had often enough and with ridiculous desperation preached that at the empty young faces. But when my boss and with him a few colleagues who wanted to ingratiate themselves expressed themselves disparagingly about my passion, I felt such a resistance rise in me against my academic courses that I was firmly determined one day to bang my fist hard on the table and no longer put up with the nastiness. Then a scornful rejection of the Hemingway showcase seemed to the staff the appropriate opportunity to run me through the gauntlet and to destroy me once and for all. In doing so they proceeded in accordance with the method that had been proven in the case of one thin-skinned colleague who a year before had died suddenly of a heart attack.

I revered *my* Hemingway. I considered him to be an outstanding writer, oblivious to the trend toward making fun of Hemingway and treating him with disdain. When an ambitiously striving colleague with the inconsiderate name of Schmitz, who had just left the trade school with a diploma, challenged me with the inquisitorial arrogance of a village policeman in front of the assembled company to state the reasons for my Hemingway showcase, Hemingway was, after all, dead, as dead as anyone could be, and *hopelessly* out, indeed, that's how he expressed himself: *hopelessly* out, I had just courteously and curtly answered with "No, thanks." Rudely, my boss had interrupted me and venomously asked me, "Then why are you sitting here? Read Brecht's *Work Journal* someday, under 'Opinions I Don't Share,' where it says that 'Hemingway has no brains.'"

"Okay, so I can leave," I had answered, had gotten up, and left without a word. I had taken my briefcase, thrown on my overcoat, and, as though it were forever, turned my back on the university bookstore. Still on my way in the direction of downtown, I had decided to give my immediate notice. Nobody could treat me that way. What had those guys been thinking of, trying to interrogate me as though in front of a judge? Not that way. Not me. I was past the age of being mobbed. I calmed down only slowly.

The houses had seemed to me like ships. Houses are ships fast at anchor, I had thought. How had that poem gone? *O my house, weigh anchor . . . into the wind of the day . . .* or something like that, or different. I had not anchored a house. Mine was floating. I was nothing more than a prematurely aging bachelor, taken care of by a Spanish cleaning woman, Señora Rodriguez, whom I sometimes called Cervantes in error, and who after more than a twenty-year sojourn in Thulsern still spoke her unique, highly personal German. It was enough to keep my apartment going. That wasn't difficult because everything that made her happy stood undisturbed in its place. And what was I? Nothing more than a bookseller at a so-called university bookstore in a provincial backwater called Thulsern, most of my gray life surrounded by ignorant female apprentice booksellers who wore torn-up gym shoes and proudly let their shirts hang out of their pants, by plotting colleagues who had for a long time made fun of me behind my back, and by books that were still my most pleasant company. I lived completely withdrawn, attended to my professional responsibilities punctually, as good as never made dates to dine out, usually declined the increasingly few invitations, got drunk alone at home, cultivated no friendships except with Mürzig, whom I seldom saw, but with whom I spoke by telephone extravagantly, put my money into books, and guarded my treasures: the shoe boxes with the clippings about Hemingway. In my leisure time I read or reflected about what I had read. Sometimes I put down my ideas neatly with my fountain pen, as I had been accustomed to doing since my youth, in one notebook or another, which I showed to no one. When you read, you are never lonely, and books, in any case, are preferable in the end to associating with disappointing people.

8

I do admit that on my numerous trips I developed a certain weakness for those unapproachably faraway, glittering songstresses who took the stage in hotel bars. With many of them I spoke over a glass or two. Many told me about their mostly unhappy lives because they knew I wanted nothing from them. Their dumb stories about men were as alike as two peas in a pod, and none of the songstresses ever refused my request for my favorite song. For me, all of them sang "Somewhere over the Rainbow." But all in all I had never been lucky with women, although in spite of everything I thought myself somewhat presentable. For a time I had dreamed of quiet happiness in a corner. I found a young woman with whom, out of complete enthusiasm for exuberant visions, I even wanted to open my own bookstore: a *real* bookstore with genuine wooden bookcases and cases with doors, only the best, not a mixed-bag bookstore as is customary today. A bookstore was for me above all a question of personal taste. But the woman was no good. Anyway, I had had to find out tediously and painfully that, in spite of her false promises and assurances, she did not love me but had merely been looking for comfortable security in her old age and had deceived me with a younger man. She was moody and undependable, always had migraines, and was always dreaming of making good, now as a highly gifted potter, now as a silk painter. She had gone along with every fashionable fad: now Chinese shadowboxing, then again archery or batik work. But she had never gotten beyond high-school level with anything. Besides, she had a propensity for picking her nose whenever she was nervous. And she was often nervous. But I would have overlooked all that if she had just been faithful to me. But she couldn't be faithful, but was fickle and unreliable.

After tormented nights, self-denials, and humiliations, I had painfully dropped this troubled romance. For a while the scars had still hurt, but then they finally healed. In the end I had just shaken my head and laughed about my own infatuation and the distortions that I had undergone for her sake. No, she had been of no use. She had even enjoyed applying makeup and looking at herself in front of the mirror for hours, then again she'd pretend to be the woman she had copied from a fashion magazine.

But actually this unhappy relationship had come apart because this young woman was not interested in reading. All the while she answered to the lovely first name of Clothilde, from which I had decided her parents must have read Adalbert Stifter's novel *Indian Summer*.

"Well, I could have liked Hemingway. That was quite a guy, a real man, broad-shouldered and full of the zest for life. But you with your books and your eternal reading," she had always reproached me with shrieking envy. "That's horribly boring. And I'm supposed to live like that? Why don't we go out sometimes or have a party? Hemingway constantly partied and enjoyed life. But we're never invited out. All that has to do with your books, with that other world that doesn't even exist. I'm repressed because you neglect me totally and love those shitty books more than you do me or anything else. No, I'm not cheating on you, as you always assume, rather you're cheating on me with your books."

At that I had hurried into my library and had taken my favorite work, which was filled with scraps of paper, and had cried out:

"Clothilde! What doesn't originate in books? Before there were books—in one form or another—before there were tales, reports, before there were words—did anything at all exist? And when thinking stops will anything at all be left? Books! What doesn't involve books? The past revives anew, memories return to life and are created again. The reality of fantasy is the fantasy of reality. The other world and that other life, as you call them, are found in this world and in this life. The famous basilisks created themselves, as Unamuno says; they disregarded blueprints and guided the hands of their maker. How often does a conscientious reader think: I once thought of that, I know that this or that thing happened to me. Simpletons however, I'm sorry, my dear, are the prisoners of suffocating banality that is concerned only with what they call probability. Or think of those who believe they live in a wakeful state as so-called realists—and all the while they don't know that only is someone really alive who has the astuteness to dream."

"Nonsense! If everything comes from books, then I would be coming from a book, too; then these writers were an excuse so that the story of their characters can be told," that silly woman had answered.

At that, in spite of her bumpy subjunctives—*came*, Clothilde, and *would come* and *would be*—I would most like to have embraced her and would have proved with the tenderest caresses that with that sentence she had understood something important; but she had warded me off, saying that I ought to have some consideration for her hairdo.

Female dirty tricks. A woman always finds something she can fight about. My God, how little a woman does know.

Clothilde thought exclusively about herself. In bed, too. She let herself be kissed, but did not return the kisses as though they might be a reply to the caresses for which she wished. She let herself be caressed, but did not caress in return, rather she stretched out her body, taken care of for hours, which wanted to be treated well. She demanded that I be nice to her but was unable to display or exhibit any kind of emotion, rather circled every loving word like a cat around a saucer of hot milk. And when it was over came the complaints: I hadn't paid attention to this and that. She was continually nagging and unsatisfied. Because she didn't have the slightest idea about reading, she also understood nothing about love and nothing about sex. She had just no imagination. Had she read more, she would have trained her power of imagination and wouldn't have lain around in bed like a machine that could be gratified only with all kinds of foolish gymnastics. Presumably she was like those American women of whom it is said in *The Short Happy Life of Francis Macomber*: *He was grateful that he had gone through his education on American women before now. . . . They are the damnedest women. Really the damnedest . . . enameled in that American female cruelty.*

I found Señora Rodriguez preferable. Of course, she didn't read either, but at least had a natural respect for the sacred relics that she so regularly and carefully dusted. And sometimes, when I watched her secretly from the side, she awakened in me the impression of a volcano that merely steams under a tightly closed lid.

Clothilde, who had been Mürzig's companion first, had become infuriated: "You're like your friend Mürzig with his repulsive mania for the subjunctive. He constantly had to correct me and always knew better. *Had* or *would have, be* or *were!* That can drive you nutty. Nothing could make him madder than bad German. Basically he corrected themes only on Saturdays, because on Sunday he had to recover from seizures produced by his pupils' errors. Then he lay completely exhausted in bed and read the classics to recuperate from the injuries done his disposition. The subjunctive was more important to him than anything. He even called my breasts subjunctive one and subjunctive two." But because of her hair-raising subjunctive mistakes he had quickly sent her to the devil and advised her to marry only a man who confused *be* and *were* wildly.

I had taken up with Clothilde back then more from pity than from affection. Of course, she looked attractive, had a pretty face, and could laugh wonderfully. My sole friend and confidant, Mürzig, had warned me urgently—"That ridiculous heart throbbing into her throat, that two-minute hot monster on her sweating skin, my dear man, and in addition to that a lifelong hangover"—but so-called love had made a clown of me, because I had paid no heed to Mürzig's advice to take a book rather than a woman to bed and become absorbed in it instead of in her.

9

In Key West I spent the night in the Overseas Hotel, where Hemingway's parents had stayed and Papa wanted to pair off his sister Sunny with John Dos Passos, whom she, however, couldn't stand because of his baldness and his fidgety movements. And then the unavoidable visit to the Hemingway House at the corner of Whitehead and Olivia Streets with a bevy of tourists in shorts and loud shirts and awesome socks that agonized through the rooms.

"Hello, everybody, nice to have you here today. . . . This is the first house that Hemingway owned. . . . In the course of the visit pictures of Hemingway's four wives will also be shown . . ."

Manuscripts have disappeared in that house. They were either stolen or chewed to pieces by mice, rats, and cockroaches. The swimming pool was disappointingly shallow.

I heard the clicking of cameras. For Hemingway the click of a camera was like the clacking of a rattlesnake. Hemingway T-shirts stretched over fat beer-and-sandwich bellies. Only, I thought I could hear another voice, as though times gone by were coming with inaudible steps up the abandoned stairs and were gliding through the corridor. The house doors ajar fascinated me particularly. With the tenderness of a blind man I wanted to stroke the book spines in the library, and a voice murmured in me: *Have a compound fracture of my index finger. Terrible wreck bear hunting. Fourteen stitches in my face, inside and out, hole in my leg, then muscle paralysis in my right arm, three fingers broken on my right hand. . . . My eyes went bad in Spain . . . then Pauline's second caesarian etc. etc.*

"All of his books reflect his experiences. Here you see a few pictures, his medals and his helmet from the First World War. That's when he met Agnes, the nurse, his first love. After that experience he wrote his book . . ."

I wanted to raise an objection and protest against that absurd thesis, but I couldn't utter a sound. In me another voice kept on talking:

What did he fear? It was not fear or dread. It was a nothing that he knew too well. It was all a nothing, and a man was nothing, too. It was only that, and light was all it needed and a certain cleanliness and order. Some lived in it and never felt it but he knew it all was nada y pues nada y nada y pues nada. *Our* nada, *who art in* nada, nada *be thy name, thy kingdom* nada, *thy will be* nada *in* nada *as it is in* nada. *Give us this* nada *our daily* nada *and* nada *us our* nada *as we* nada *our* nadas *and* nada *us not into* nada *but deliver us from* nada; pues nada. *Hail full of nothing, nothing is with thee.*

I stared at a gleaming espresso maker and on the counter found the brass plate with Hemingway's name: a tourist attraction, a sale article. Hemingway's face looked at me even from the beer coasters.

Sloppy Joe's Bar.

Hemingway's Favorite Bar.

People were standing neck by jowl, being as noisy as an army of penguins. I talked about boxing with an old man who looked like a film star, had the protruding belly of a drinker, the neck of a turtle, hair as though licked by a cow, skipping on short legs and letting his bear paws dangle: "Ernest wanted to be the champion. He also often talked about writing in the jargon of boxers. I then went into a crouch and hit him with my left always on the same spot.

Right in his mouth. All of a sudden it was full of blood. He turned around and spit on me. I was splattered with blood from head to toe. I was horrified and didn't know whether I had hit him hard. When he saw my dumbfounded face, he cried out: Everything's okay. That's what bullfighters do to show their disdain. Then he laughed. Most of the time he was in control of himself. Once or twice he beat people up who provoked him when he was tipsy. When drunks bothered him at parties he reacted at once. Once when we were having a drink, a drunk came up and said: 'Hey, Hemingway!' The reaction was a quick right to the guy's chin so that he flew over three tables into the corner. The incident was a feast for the gossip columns: *Hemingway again involved in a drunken brawl!* But it was just a punch that put a pushy drunk out of action. But he had to put up with such articles his whole life."

10

A thick haze hung in the bar. And already my thoughts were wandering back. Every Saturday evening I filled up a zinc bathtub with a few buckets of lukewarm water for Grandmother. Then Grandmother appeared in the kitchen in her nightgown, and I accompanied the old woman down into the preheated wash-house, supporting her from stair step to stair step, watching out for every one of her steps on the coconut runner, finally took away her cane, put it on the seat of the chair on which a washcloth already lay, helped the body, dry as a fence post, first onto a low stool, finally into the tub. My grandmother tested the temperature of the water with her left foot, played a bit in it with her toes, nodded in satisfaction, and smiled. That was the signal to help her completely into the tub, which stood in the washhouse like a canoe. Then I turned around quickly, heard Grandmother pulling her nightgown over her head, let her lay it over my arm—my gaze fixed steadily on the door—tucked the nightgown as carefully as a wedding gown over the chair back, put the washcloth ready, and finally heard grandmother letting herself sink totally into the water. Without looking around, I knew that the old woman disappeared in the steam. Quickly I left the wash-house, quickly shut the door so that no warmth would get out, for Grandmother easily got a chill. While I was going up the stairs into the apartment, two steps at a time, I imagined Grandmother's washing ritual, saw how one hand looked for the bath salts, heard the green paper of the pine needle tablets crackle, saw how her old hand pulverized the tablets before the grains were scattered into the water, swirled it up, let the fizz foam. Now it was the turn of the preserve jar with the dried weeds: hay buds. Grandmother swore on the healing power of hay buds. And on a small bowl of lemon balm. For circulation. Stir everything together slowly, taking a deep breath all the while, and nestle down into the tub. Every Saturday evening.

Every Saturday evening, meanwhile, upstairs in the

parlor I prepared the chair in which Grandmother would sit after her bath. I spread the blanket over it, so that Grandmother could wrap herself up in it and wouldn't catch a chill. I knew that every detail had to be taken heed of, for Grandmother put great value in that. Nothing should irritate her. For that reason the little blanket, against which the old woman would soon lay her head, should also lie upon the wing chair.

I imagined Grandmother washing herself. I saw the washcloth move over the thin legs, carefully along the varicose veins that like fat worms wound around her calves. And I visualized how the curd soap went between her legs, up and down her upper thighs, along her hips, circling around her stomach, under her breasts and over the breasts to her neck, lingering long at her neck and from there to her armpits, until finally her face was next. Maybe the soap slipped out of her hand once, perhaps it disappeared in the hay buds and the lemon balm, perhaps she would catch it again, slippery as a trout. Perhaps she would rinse with the little spouted pot—this was particularly nice around the shoulders and down the back. Perhaps long, thin fingers with short nails gripped the rounded rim of the tub, perhaps the stringy arms would lift the old body energetically upward. Then came the grab for the hand towel, the careful drying and rubbing, gingerly around the varicose veins. From below upward for the circulation of the blood. And then the shivering, causing goose bumps that are yellow and pale. Only her arms are brown, up to the elbows. Finally the nightgown was slipped on and tied lightly over her breasts. Her feet slid into slippers.

As soon as she had finished her ablutions, Grandmother knocked with her cane against the wooden ceiling of the washhouse. That was the signal for me to run down the steep staircase that had the coconut runner, two steps at a time, open the washhouse door, and fetch Grandmother. Every Saturday evening the vapor of hay buds and pine needles and lemon balm and old woman struck me. A spouted pot was floating on the tub water. Grandmother smiled, told me to open the screen to let the mist out. Then Grandmother laid her hand on my shoulder and supported herself on me. She was tall and thin. She maintained that earlier she had been a stately woman and liked to point to a brownish photograph in a wooden frame. It showed a proud woman with a bun, dressed in something black with cuffs and pointed collar and a low waist. Before I accompanied Grandmother to the door and up the steep stairs, I had still to take the washcloth out of the water, hang it next to a board-stiff hand towel on the line, on which still other washcloths were hanging like dead birds. With the spouted pot I scooped up the lemon balm and the hay buds. Only then did I pull the plug from the bottom of the tub and let the water run out gurgling. If only the stairs up to the parlor had not been so steep, if only it didn't always take so much time. First a foot, then the cane. On the way I said to Grandmother, while she was wheezing, for such a bath was an exertion, that she smelled fragrant. She liked to hear that. Then it was easier to go on again. We took our time until we arrived at the parlor, and it took a while still until Grandmother sank with a groan into the chair, pulled up her legs, set her feet on the little footstool, and let me wrap her up in the blanket. Old speckled hands held the blanket, played with the fringe, plucked loose ends. Then the hands wandered to her head and felt for the bun, tested it with practiced grasps, stroked one strand behind her ear, all the hairpins were in place. Grandmother breathed regularly. She could do that only when she knew that her hair bun was all right. She needed that certainty. She had always seen to it that everything was fine with the bun and with all else. Her eyelids got heavier. And how heavy they got! All her years were hanging suddenly on her eyelids. It became more and more difficult for Grandmother to keep her eyes open. What an effort that cost her. But she didn't give up. However, finally she did resign herself to it. Her eyes showed me what weight resignation can have. Grandmother sat in her wing chair as on a throne. Then she began to speak. First were the directions about how the house was to be kept clean, where I should dust first, where the dust liked to collect particularly, what had not been polished for far too long, even the curtains had to be washed once more and the kitchen urgently to be whitewashed, how long the gutters had not been cleaned out, it must look devastating in the attic, what a disgrace, if someone were to come. But nobody came. And then Grandmother would sail through the swamps of the past. She spoke with eyes closed, as in sleep. I didn't budge from the spot, watched lips that had become thin, and quivering nostrils, studied the trembling of small facial hairs, and the twitching of the leathery skin of her face. She had owned all the records by Caruso, Grandmother told me, and a bitter grimace came over her mouth. She had seen so many into the grave who had preceded her. And she told about the big house of a public health officer where she had been employed and had polished champagne buckets, all the table silver, and the candelabra. Even the winding of the clocks had taken hours. And while Grandmother slipped into slumber, I rummaged in my Hemingway shoe box.

11

I n his birthplace at the gates of Chicago, Oak Park,
Illinois, which Hemingway had characterized as a
place of *wide lawns and narrow minds,* at 339 North
Oak Park Avenue I found the house in which he was born,
between Victorian houses with dark and cornered gables and
across the street from a Methodist church, and Hemingway's
name on a memorial tablet on the house, set by the
Historical Society of Oak Park and River Forest, 1974.

In Oak Park in the summer, in the middle of the July
heat, there is a *Fiesta de Hemingway,* established by the
local Hemingway Foundation. Beer-drinking daddies push
baby carriages with their bellies, clowns paint children's

faces, flamenco dancers stomp on plank floors, from a podium young lyric poets declaim their latest endeavors. Numerous people dress up like the residents of Pamplona when the bulls run through the streets. But the bulls in Oak Park aren't real. They are coffin-like boxes on a chassis with two wheels, a wooden skull from which enormous horns jut out. These coffins are pushed by screaming women and girls who romp along behind the men and drive them through the streets. *The fun also rises.* They have established a museum and renovated a classroom in the Oak Park–River Forest High School so they can plan a class reunion of old school chums. But the high point is the Hemingway look-alike contest, where anyone can try to win a box of cigars (*Tampas* or *Fannie May*), a certificate, or a Hemingway T-shirt, presented by Margaux Hemingway, the celebrated model-actress. *Think you look like Ernie? Check out this contest. Contestants are asked to dress in recognizable Hemingway or period garb and make a one-minute presentation relative to the age or experiences they represent in Hemingway's life.*

And what do people say about all that? Some swear that Hemingway would have enjoyed it immensely, others are convinced that he would have hated it. One of the people said: "Anyway, he would have had a drink."

Whatever, Oak Park celebrates. Every year all over

again. The newspapers are full of articles about *The Young Man* and *The Suburb* and *The Oak Park Years*. And all are unanimous: *Come Home, Papa. All Is Forgiven.* It hasn't been so long ago that his works were still sold in the bookstores under the counter.

Oak Park: a bitter disappointment, apparently a place without secrets, banal in its normality; no more and no less than just any American Nowheresville.

I thought of the young Hemingway in the Field Museum of Natural History in the hall with the African mammals in front of cheetahs, lions, warthogs, buffalo, and hyenas. I imagined the glimmer of the glass eyes in the dimmed light of the cases, and I knew how much that had impressed the boy. But there was something else that I imagined in the public library: *We grew up very religious with morning prayers in which even the housemaid and the cook participated. Usually we sat in the living room, Father read from the prayer book, and my sister Ursula played the hymns. Fifty cents was paid for every new song we memorized.* And a school friend recalled: *When I visited him in Michigan, we went fishing. I had never before caught trout, so he had to show me how. When I caught more than he, I wasn't allowed to tell anyone about it. He just wanted to be the best.* The *Kansas City Star* had become a different newspaper. And its style sheet of the time no longer counted: *Write strong declarative sentences. Avoid trite adjectives. Use short sentences. Be positive, not negative.* Today different rules and tastes are valid in literature, and Hemingway's style is merely smiled at arrogantly by young writers. Disparagingly it is said that Hemingway was like pasted-on chest hair.

I reread Hemingway's letters from that period: *Today I had three articles in the* Star. *Seems to be a pretty good newspaper. They have a large editorial staff. I start work mornings at 8 and quit at 5 in the afternoon and have Saturday off. There was something to do every minute in the past few weeks. A large barn burned. I got there about the same time as the fire dept. and helped carry the hose up on the roof and had a good time generally. This last week I have been handling a murder story. Now, dry those tears Mother and cheer up. Don't worry or cry or fret about my not being a good Christian. So cheer up! Just because I'm a cheerful Christian ought not to bother you. Love—Ernie.*

In one of the numerous churches in Oak Park I prayed for all that I wanted and feared never to get. And thought about Hemingway and how he turned Catholic. When he had problems with Pauline in bed and nothing more would help, the pious Catholic woman advised him to go to church and pray. And behold: it worked again. But maybe Hemingway also turned Catholic only because all the Spanish bullfighters are Catholics.

In the local newspaper I came across a picture. It showed an eighty-seven-year-old man who had set his car and his house on fire. His marriage had reached its apex. On the evening before, his wife had returned from a visit with her daughter in Lawrence, Kansas, and had found the front door locked. Nevertheless she got into the house through the door to the backyard. Her husband got so mad about it that he struck her with a heavy electric cord. The back of her head was hurt pretty badly. Finally, she succeeded in running to a neighbor. At that the old man poured gallons of gasoline all over the house and in the garage, didn't spare the rabbit warren, and set fire to everything. It took eight firemen to subdue the man. Nothing could be saved.

I drove into the woods on the northern peninsula of Michigan near the little town of Seney, about fifteen miles from the upper lake where Hemingway had fished in the summer of 1919.

A local resident offered to take me to the place where Hemingway had gone after trout. However, what we found was the slimy brew of a poisoned river that toiled through a stinking trash dump.

He felt he had left everything behind, the need for thinking, the need to write, other needs. It was all in back of him.

From there on to Cody, Wyoming. But there were no more grizzly bears. The people on the ranch told about an army chaplain who went hunting for boar with his friend, the chief ranger. The two men, who had known one another since being prisoners of war in Europe, had to climb up a snow-covered hill. Both men lost their footing. The army chaplain's rifle went off and hit the ranger in the head. He was dead on the spot. The ranger was buried with military honors, and his friend and murderer read the funeral mass.

The journey continued on to Toronto, where Hemingway worked for the *Toronto Star*. The topics of the young journalist ranged from trembling sensitivity to an obsession with violence, from "How Do I Borrow an Oil Painting" to "The Risks of a Free Shave at the Local Barber School."

12

In the summer when everything started, in addition to reading short stories I also got used to smoking a pipe because I felt it flattered me and made me more mature. I bought a pipe with a broad bowl, which wasn't exactly cheap, and a fifty-gram can of sweet tobacco that, according to its label, tasted like some exotic fruit or other. I chose that taste mainly because of the can. I liked it because it depicted a fine, full-bearded gentleman in a black suit, a half-length picture just big enough for a locket, and over that it read: *Pipe Smoker's Sunday*. Grandmother had nothing against my smoking. She just looked pleased and for her part lit a small cigar, as she always did when she finished her work and took a seat on her chair to lay out the cards.

But maybe everything began with a picture of Hemingway in the readers' circle. It showed Papa with a billed cap, relaxing next to his nine-year-old son Gregory on a wooden bridge, one hand on his bent right knee, his gaze fixed skeptically in the distance. Papa wears a fisherman's vest with huge pockets and cartridge flaps, two buttons are buttoned, making it a bit tight across his chest, and he is wearing high fisherman's boots that he has turned down over his calves. The boy lies beside him, barefoot, with eyes almost closed, casually cradling with an open hand one of the two rifles next to him. I stared as though electrified at the picture, couldn't get enough of it. And the more ardently I stared at the picture and crept into it, the more I imagined that I was the boy. I was able to think myself into the picture to such an extent that I heard the wind in the willows on the riverbank and saw how the grass moved with a whisper. I imagined that I was dog tired because I had been hunting with Papa. And I imagined how he initiated me into the rules and secrets of the hunt and how I felt when I fired my first shot. I still felt the recoil of the rifle on my shoulder, but it was a pain that made me proud because I knew that I had now learned a part of life that was inseparably bound with death. Papa called that *the gift of death*. And he knew it well.

I believe he knew it like no one else in the world. *He had his own standards when it came to shooting.* My denim pants are frayed, and I prop myself with bare heels on the planks of the bridge. In the background the river flows sluggishly. The opposite side of the river is not far away. Papa has wrinkled his brow and squinted his eyes a little. But we make a peaceful picture, although I don't know what goes on in Papa's head. He somehow looks happy, but not entirely. And I think he was never completely happy, even when he beamed at times. There was always a residue of sadness, skepticism, or seriousness that nested between his eyes or in the wrinkles of his brow. Anyway, I am very tired. And very happy.

I was crazy about another readers' circle photograph of Hemingway. It showed Papa in the snow. He's walking along a plowed road, in the background fields covered with deep snow and snow-covered mountains. It must have been a foggy day when the picture was taken, for the clouds hang low over the forested slopes. So Papa is marching along the road. He wears a large-checkered shirt and a vest that is closed up to his neck with a zipper. It is the vest with the big chest pocket on the left side that I already knew from other pictures. And naturally an unavoidable Papa-cap sits on his head, pulled far down over his brow. Papa has incredible boots on his feet, boots with an absolutely incredible tread: as though he were about to go into the ice. The snapshot was taken at the exact second when Papa kicked up an empty beer can lying on the road. For that reason he is balancing with his left foot on tiptoe, while the other leg kicks out at almost a ninety-degree angle, and the boots show their incredible sole tread. The beer can is suspended at an angle high in the air. It must have been a bull's eye: *This was,* he said, *the best picture I ever had taken.*

My grandmother was holding a readers' circle that was brought and exchanged every week by a war widow named Mrs. Fritz. The readers' circle consisted of a bundle of various kinds of illustrated magazines that reported on fashion, film stars, and what we considered high society at the time. There were endless stories about Soraya and Brigitte Bardot, about the private lives of politicians, and about the crowned heads who had not yet died out. The older the magazines were, the less they cost. And since my grandmother had to count her pennies, she was among the last to receive the readers' circle. That didn't bother us a whit. On the contrary, Grandmother gulped up the horoscope and compared the predictions with how it had really been weeks before, and I clipped for myself all the pictures of Hemingway that I could find. I plastered the walls of my room with them. Best of all I liked the picture in which Papa is holding a cat in his hands. It imbued me with confidence in my own future, and Grandmother liked the picture, too. Since the magazines were full of Hemingway photographs back then, I soon had a respectable collection that, since the walls of my room were quickly papered with them, I saved in a shoe box. It wasn't long until I owned a real archive. In addition, I hadn't rested until I, too, had located a billed cap like the one Hemingway wore. I would most of all like to have written *Papa* on the front in big letters with a ballpoint pen, but Grandmother persuaded me not to and warned me of possibly being teased. So I didn't do it, since I wasn't keen about fights and taunts. I had enough of that in school, where because of my rather weak constitution, above all in sports, I was constantly exposed to the hatefulness of my schoolmates. I hated gymnastics on any kind of apparatus and the shot put. In soccer I was a complete failure. I could run only a little; my fear had taught me that quite early. Fears by the ton. I had been afraid since I could remember. I believe I never spent a day in my whole life without being afraid. Fear never left my side: *that cold, eroding fear, like a cold, slimy hole in all the emptiness.* But for all practical purposes I went to bed wearing my cap. With it I felt peaceful and strong, and that was important in those days. The cap and

Grandmother's unshakable affection sheltered me from all attacks. *Were it not for being afraid, every shoeshine boy in Spain would be a bullfighter.* To this very day I haven't parted with the billed cap.

My reverence for Hemingway, who seemed to me invincible and whom I chose to be my friend, my protector, indeed, even my father, went so far that I even christened my cat, which up to then was called simply Cat, Hemingway because it, too, was such an inexhaustible hunter. Best of all, if that had been possible, I would have adopted Hemingway as my father. The cat seemed to be indifferent to all of that, for unheeding its new, honorable name, it came and went as it liked.

I would like very much to have been the way his friends saw Hemingway: . . . *wearing khaki pants held up by a wide old leather belt with a huge buckle inscribed GOTT MIT UNS—*he had taken it from a dead Nazi—*a white linen sport shirt that hung loose, and brown leather loafers without socks. His hair was dark, with gray highlights, flecked white at the temples, and he had a heavy moustache that ran past the corners of his mouth, but no beard. He was massive. Not in height, for he was only an inch over six feet, nor in weight, but in impact. Most of his two hundred pounds was concentrated above his waist: he had square heavy shoulders,* *long, hugely muscled arms (the left one jaggedly scarred and a bit misshapen at the elbow), a deep chest, a belly-rise but no hips or thighs. Something played off him—he was intense, electrokinetic, but in control, a racehorse reined in. . . . —* enjoyment: *God, I thought, how he's enjoying himself! . . . He radiated it and everyone in the place responded.*

Yes, I would like to have been like that also. But if I couldn't be, because I was too young and was too afraid of everything and everybody, then at least my father should be like that. I never felt at ease in my own skin—except when I was reading. And when I was reading Hemingway, I myself became Hemingway. My longing to admire the writer even because of his mistakes and his weaknesses remained insatiable. I needed that.

13

When a new readers' circle arrived, I pounced on it and, as always, looked for stories about Hemingway, about whom a long series was being published. I read everything that had to do with him with feverish attention. I was electrified especially by one thing:

In the winter of 1922 the American writer Ernest Hemingway was living in Paris with his first wife, Hadley. During his trips the writer and journalist often left his wife at home. Shortly before Christmas of 1922 he was staying in Lausanne to report on an international conference for a newspaper. He wanted to meet Hadley in Lausanne and then go to Chamby skiing with her, above Montreux. When Hadley followed him to Lausanne, she wanted to surprise her husband and so took along all his manuscripts, so that he could work on them evenings during their skiing holiday. In a small suitcase she packed everything that he had written up to that time. The handwritten originals, the typed manuscripts, and the carbon copies. At the Gare de Lyon she had her luggage taken to a compartment by a baggage carrier. She stowed the large travel bag in the luggage net, the smaller suitcase she left lying on the seat. She left the compartment and conversed on the platform with a few friendly journalists who had brought her to the train. When she returned to the compartment, the suitcase with the manuscripts had vanished. Hadley searched through several compartments and asked the newspaper people for advice, but the suitcase remained missing. It was never found. When Hadley arrived in Lausanne, she hardly dared tell Hemingway what had happened. He raged and immediately took the train back to Paris to see for himself whether she had been mistaken and had at least left the carbon copies in the apartment. But everything he had written up to then was gone: twenty or more stories, a novel begun, and some sketches. A couple of things were safe. One story had by chance been sent to a magazine, another manuscript had slid down behind the sofa and Hadley had not noticed it while packing the suitcase. Hemingway had buried the manuscript of "Up in Michigan" in a drawer because Gertrude Stein had not liked it. But the remainder never turned up. Hemingway never forgave his wife for the missing suitcase, and the unfortunate incident—as the biographers can report—is said to have been in the end one of the main reasons for the divorce from Hadley. As Hemingway remarked in a letter to Ezra Pound, Hadley had "done a good job of it," while Pound called the affair "a work of God" and advised Hemingway to rewrite the material from memory, that "best critic." He himself never disclosed anything about the details of that night. Maybe he got drunk and went to a whore, maybe he thought about suicide. The next morning he went straight to Gertrude Stein and Alice B. Toklas, who were very sympathetic and fixed him a good lunch. On the return trip to Lausanne that same evening he drank a large bottle of Beaune in the dining car.

I couldn't get the matter of the suitcase that was never found out of my head. I imagined all kinds of stories that lay in the suitcase, but above all I imagined the suitcase itself: brown leather, already somewhat worn and scratched, with a good handle and two straps for reinforcement. I knew that somewhere the suitcase was waiting to be opened, I knew that someone had the suitcase, and I resolved to look for it one day, if I had enough money to circle the world on the search for Papa's suitcase. "God sends nuts, but He doesn't crack them," my grandmother said to that. The more I dreamed about the suitcase, the more real it became and the more certain I was that I really would find it one day. From my mental images and wishful thinking I literally read it into being.

I immediately got the school atlas and wrote down the places where Hemingway had sojourned. I noted the names of the hotels that came up in the articles in the illustrated magazines, I acquired an extra notebook for all my notes and records: *Ambos Mundos*, Havana; *Stanley Hotel*, Nairobi; *Florida Gaylord* and *Suecia*, Madrid; *Hotel Majestic*, Barcelona; *Dorchester*, London; *Villa Aprile*, Cortina d'Ampezzo; *Hôtel de Cité*, Carcassonne; *Hotel Quintana*, Pamplona. In addition came names such as Venice and Key West.

Nothing but magical places.

14

I was standing in front of an antiquarian bookstore. My steps had led me automatically to this store, for I had always had a weakness for old and sequestered books. Antiquarian bookstores exuded an irresistible attraction for me. I suffered from an illness called bibliomania.

Untiringly I had repeated my advice to the apprentices at the book-trade school that they should acquire their own libraries in the course of time and become their own librarians: "Borges always imagined Paradise to be a kind of library. In a library treasures are not only collected, catalogued, and displayed—in a library you can measure the intellectual pulse of your own time, if you will allow me this worn-out metaphor. From a library you can travel over the whole world and see more than the greatest explorers. With aesthetic charm comes moral responsibility. A library is, so to speak, tradition turned into reality; and fidelity is its highest law, for tradition is not a dead chapter. Casanova, for example, wrote in his memoirs about the library at Wolfenbüttel: 'I spent eight days in this library, which I left only to go to my inn to eat and to sleep. I can count those eight days among the happiest of my life, for I wasn't occupied with myself for a moment; I thought neither of the past nor the future, and my mind, which had been immersed completely in my work, could not remark the present. Since then I have at times thought that the lives of the saints could be something similar.' A good reader is always also a discoverer or a rediscoverer of forgotten or overlooked books. Seek and ye shall find! That saying is made truth nowhere more than in a library. Decisive therein is unpremeditated searching. Practice the art of reading at random! You will never come out of a library without profit, no matter how small it is. Every book represents an intellectual harvest, the collected power of an author that is within reach even after his death. Without the memorable feasts of the power of imagination, for which we are grateful to libraries as storehouses, we would, every one of us, be as insipid as an old hound dog."

And finally I had called out to my bewildered listeners, future booksellers: "Think of the Cabala, whose readers proceed from the assumption that behind every word lies a second, hidden meaning. Everything must be understood twofold because there is another mystery in prophesying. Ladies and gentlemen, do not listen to the objections of those who confuse the bookworm with the bibliomaniac or assert the mania for reading to be a plague, worse than the yellow fever of Philadelphia. They are the mighty who fear the powerless versed in reading when they say: *Since the maid has been reading novels, civic integrity is regretfully absent.* Our fault finders speak like the blind do of color. Ancient wisdom, ladies and gentlemen! It waits for you, and for you, and for you! Therefore I advise you urgently, as your old Hemingstein, whom you smile at with pity: Read, ladies and gentlemen, for God's sake, read, otherwise you will have to become critics."

In all other ways I was a human being like any other. But as soon as books were involved, I was as though transformed: a fundamentalist. For me, a bibliography consisted not merely of a boring list of titles but of the dimly badgering expectation of unexpected pleasures. I had an understanding for everyone whom bibliomania misled to murder. And, like all bibliomaniacs, I had an unhappy inclination toward stinginess. That circumstance led me to avoid public auctions, where, as a bibliomaniac, one can be ruined beyond recall. Instead, I eagerly visited those small shops where I spent little but in return had the pleasure of being able to rummage thoroughly. Bibliomania is one of the strongest passions when it is turned loose. For that reason I could never stop visiting antiquarian bookstores. I knew every superstition of the dealers, their prejudices and tricks. But surrounded by the odor of mold and rags, I always had the happiest moments of my life.

Without hesitation, and with my own untamable dark rage at my boss and my colleagues in my belly, I had stepped into the shop and, to quell my reaction to my anger completely, indeed, to do something good after the humiliation that had been done me, I reached for the nearest book. I already had thumbed through the pages and let the seductive aroma rise in my nose. Finally I had looked at the cover and seen that the book coincidentally was concerned with a work on Hemingway that had remained unknown to me. Thereupon I had again turned to the page that had been held by my thumb. And standing I had begun to read the passage:

In the winter of 1922 the American writer Ernest Hemingway was living in Paris with his first wife, Hadley. During his trips the writer and journalist often left his wife at home. Shortly before Christmas of 1922 he was staying in Lausanne to report on an international conference for a newspaper. He wanted to meet Hadley in Lausanne and then go to Chamby skiing with her, above Montreux. When Hadley followed him to Lausanne, she wanted to surprise her husband and so took along all his manuscripts . . .

I needed to read no further. It was the story of Papa's suitcase, which I had already read years before in my grandmother's readers' circle. I remembered every word, and the old fever broke out anew. This time more powerful than before.

In my place, I thought, Hemingway would have stood up at the staff meeting and, with a well-placed right hook, would have laid out my superior on the felt carpet of the conference room for a while. Hemingway would have done that—but how shabbily had I acted? I had just gotten up and left. No, Hemingway would not have put up with that kind of effrontery. He would have acted. He would have acted like a man. Abruptly I had imagined how he would have lit into my boss, how he would have jabbed his fist in his musical-comedy gangster's mug so that his teeth grated, how my boss would have rolled his eyes and wouldn't have been able to hold his bloody spit, how the boss would have folded up like a pocket knife, finally to strike the floor with his rattling skull. And immediately after that, Papa would have given that beardless youth—what was his name? Schmitz, yeah, Schmitz—a dressing down.

I slammed the book shut, went right to the cashier—and in doing so almost made a pile of books sway—paid without a word, put the book into my briefcase, and left the antiquarian bookstore with the knowledge of again having set the switch for my future life with the purchase of the Hemingway biography. Hardly had I left the store when my thoughts digressed. My right fist was hurting.

15

I had been invited to a birthday party that evening. My
old friend and sole confidant, Assistant Principal
Mürzig, had recited a witty story. It had been a successful and entertaining birthday party because the birthday
boy, a young colleague of Mürzig's, who had financed his
studies as a cabdriver, had wished the well-wishers to give
him stories as presents. I had listened attentively and
reflected for a long time about Mürzig's annotations:

"Recently it could be read," Mürzig had said, with a
serious expression on his face, "that a letter in a bottle was
washed up on the beach of Huka-Niva in the middle of the
Pacific Ocean. It was said that it contained old stories. Just a

conjecture. For the writing could no longer be deciphered. The so-called stories had evidently been written with an ink that had been mixed magically with such cleverness that after a few months it had already faded. Today many stories turn out to be stolen, others to be lost. They no longer exist. So it's the end of stories. The blame for that lies in the hole in the ozone layer, the fluctuation in the price of the yen, the motor-driven carving knife. So, finished, gone. In a few Alpine valleys they say even today on occasion: *If it happens, it happens!* But nothing at all *happens*. So even there stories are done for. If you wanted to revive the tradition of such stories, you would have to invent some. But you're frequently too lazy or too short on ideas for that. So you never mind it. It's over with stories. Most have fizzled out. Occasionally a story does still happen, here or there. Then it is often called a fine story, with the emphasis on *fine*. Usually it has to do with the story of two lovers. But what comes out in the end is hardly more than lechery between people dependent on one another. We can do without that. Now and then we hear of stories that are supposed to have described life. All sheer nonsense. Life is a stranger to writing. It lashes out at best. And that's okay. If you agree with Mr. Hemingway in that regard, then the best stories are without exception by Mark Twain. Hemingway was a good

81

fisherman. Besides that, we know that he called Marlene Dietrich 'the Kraut.' Otherwise everything revolved around sound and fury, master and dog, fool and death, mountains, seas, and giants, Snow White and Rose Red, fortune like glass, you don't say, plastic and elastic. Stories are the mending of art, the embroidery of holes, nothing more. The most beautiful and the truest of stories can today be experienced in an elevator, when the cabined persons turn as one toward the automatic door instead of looking one another in the eye or grabbing at one another's pockets. Some people proclaim to this very day that one may not—because of inherent Utopia and also because writing, good writing, meant always writing against something—one may never stop inventing stories. That's nonsense. I've never caught sight of Lady Utopia. Presumably, somewhere in Bangkok, she sells fumigating candles. Instead of that: brands of foodstuff! That's an unadulterated story. Many so-called stories remain a fragment. In that regard anything can become a story. Any affliction becomes bearable, if it can be recast as a story. And no story is told only a single time."

At the name Hemingway the glass in my hand had trembled, and it had seemed to me as though I had been awakened from a dream.

16

At the hotel in Oak Park I watched the local news. There was a report told about a twenty-two-year-old man who wanted to go to a cookout but because of his drunken condition was tossed out. The soldier and weapons fanatic cursed the guests and threatened them with a jackknife. He goes home, gets a pistol, and shoots his sleeping parents to death. Then he goes back to the party and starts shooting wildly at random. Three young men are dead on the spot, one dies later, a woman receives life-threatening wounds. The other guests at the party, screaming, take flight outside. The marksman flees from the police, who have been summoned, and starts a gun fight in which two policemen are seriously wounded. In the morning hours in the course of a large search the young man is found dead on a park bench. He has shot himself in the mouth.

I continue my travels to Horton Bay in northern Michigan, where Hemingway and Hadley were married on the third of September, 1921. Hadley had appeared at the church fifteen minutes late. That afternoon she had gone swimming and had underestimated the time she would need to dry her hair.

Nobody in Horton Bay could remember the wedding, but they did remember a young man who poured gasoline over a seven-year-old girl and set her afire out of rage and sadness that his girlfriend, the child's mother, was about to leave him. First he drove around the area aimlessly in his car with the child. He stopped at a field lane. He gathered some wood and twigs, stacked it up, laid the child on top, poured gasoline on it, and set it on fire. Afterward, he drove away. Their attention caught by the plumes of smoke, two field workers discovered the child, but at first thought a doll was involved.

17

U p to that time there had been only one magical place for me: Thulsern's *Spa Movies* and the posters at the entrance. There in the window hung the pictures of my heroes: robust faces, brave, defiant young women, captains of the economic miracle, and noble forest rangers. Whenever these pictures return to my memory, they then start to move, and nothing makes sense anymore. They melt into a single film, which I saw again and again during the time I was growing up. Liesl, the girl from the city, goes walking through the Silver Woods with the forest ranger Hubert, who later becomes an insurance salesman. The pair of lovers Anna and Rolf row over the heath lake. From the shore sounds the merry song of three vagabonds. Good people walk through robust natural surroundings in which stags bellow and narcissus blooms. Sonya Ziemann loves Rudolf Prack, who quarrels with Paul Hörbiger, but Sonya Ziemann wins a car in the *tombola*, a former lord of the manor turns into a poacher, a mean animal keeper needs meat for his circus lions, and the residents on the heath celebrate a shooting match. The brutal farmer Eschmann courts the farmer's daughter Dorothee. But the lover of her youth returns from the city. Eschmann is consumed by jealousy and stalks Dorothee. He lies in wait for her, she tries to get away but gets lost on the moor, where Eschmann attacks her. Then comes a flashback to the Thirty Years' War. The Swedish captain has been smitten by a young virgin who wants to have nothing to do with him. She lures him onto the moor, pretends to succumb to his demands, but he ravishes her (as they said back then), and both sink in the moor. But the village is saved. Roses blossom on the heath grave, and Liane, the girl from the primeval forest, lives with the tribe of the Wodos. She wears almost nothing and her breasts can be seen from the side, for which reason you go to the movie twice. Presumably she is the granddaughter of the Hamburg shipowner Amelongen. So she is caught in a net by Hardy Krüger and taken directly from the primeval forest to Hamburg, where the managing director Schönick already sees his chance swimming off into the distance. In any case, it was he who rebuilt the enterprise from the rubble after the war. And that's going to be taken away from him through the inheritance of the naked jungle girl. Schönick murders Amelongen, but Liane, for whom the way seems clear, returns to the primeval forest with Hardy Krüger because things there are more unsullied than in Hamburg. In Berlin Professor Sauerbruch performs surgery here and there on Heidemarie Hatheyer, although she has no money. In addition, the privy counselor also heals a dog. But Dieter Borsche, on the other hand, leads a double life. Heavy guilt burdens him. In the Russian prisoner-of-war camp he had successfully performed a difficult operation, although he had not finished his medical training. Back in Germany his grateful patient gets him a post as head doctor. But on the side, in the stealth of night, Borsche must make up his examinations. As head doctor he is with the manufacturer's daughter, but as a perpetual student he's the friend of Ruth Leuwerick. One fine day he can no longer endure the conflicts of his conscience and turns himself in, but he is released and gets Leuwerick, whom O. W. Fischer—formerly King Ludwig—could not have because she was the empress of Austria and already married. So Ruth Leuwerick goes to a nunnery. But there she is taken on by baron von Trapp, a former submarine captain, as a nursemaid, for the baron's wicked children have already driven several governesses to desperation. Finally the baron marries the novice, while the family pastor, Josef Meinrad, gathers the children as well as the mother into a choir, for where song is, there you can abide. Because she is clever and at the peak of her life, Lady Leuwerick in the twinkling of an eye makes a hotel out of the palace. While the Nazis march into Austria and the eastern province returns home to the Reich, the Trapp family emigrates to America, where they are loved because they wear peasant dresses and lederhosen. As the daughter of an American millionaire, Lady Leuwerick returns to the Grand Duchy of Grimmburg, which again is being ruled by Dieter Borsche. As a good German, he learns from her what democracy is; she in turn moves up to high nobility like Grace Kelly in Monaco and understands finally how important tradition and history are, which, as is well known, do not exist in America.

I grew up in this backwoods idyll. And the stories of Hemingway smashed it like a meteorite. I never had very many friends and avoided the usual cliques. There were only a few with whom I undertook to do anything together, for I was a loner from the start. All my reading sort of brought that about. As did my fear. Two can't read together, that's something that can be done only in solitude. Sometimes I met Berni, who lived not far from us. Berni was a stout boy with strong arms. He was ten months older than I, and he was fairly hard on himself and on others. His parents were doctors. And sometimes Berni's mother let him drive her car, an old Volkswagen. Secretly, on the country roads, because Berni did not have a driver's license.

18

Somewhere on the search for Papa's suitcase I read in the newspaper in a hotel lobby a long article by a lady journalist, who despised Hemingway, the man and the writer, and in her disparaging remarks supported her views by citing an American historian named Lynn from the Johns Hopkins University in Baltimore.

The woman called Hemingway a ruin, a prematurely aged wreck, a mother's boy, a latent queer with constant anxiety about impotence. She said those things with an offhandedness as though she were cracking a peanut shell. While she, with the grace of a crab, charged the writer with all kinds of defamations—he had maligned F. Scott

Fitzgerald, he had persecuted Ford Madox Ford malevolently, and he had *literally blackened* John Dos Passos's character by saying he had Negro blood—the journalist left out none of her *dirty tricks*. No wonder: She was earning money as a literary critic.

Hemingway called the critics "eunuchs of literature." From him came the statements: *Only a dead critic is a good critic. Reviews are about as interesting and constructive as other people's laundry lists. Criticism is like horse shit but without horse shit's pleasant smell nor use as fertilizer. Most compliments are horse shit, too. Critics do not know their ass from a hole in the ground. I do not know one I would want with me, or trust with me, if we ever had to fight for anything. All reviews are shit. Criticism is getting all mixed up with a combination of the junior FBI-men, discards of Freud and Jung, and a sort of columnist-peephole. Having books published is very destructive to writing, and then to read the reviews. If they don't understand it, they become furious, and that doesn't do you any good*

Professor Lynn, the informant for the journalists, was not a biographer after my taste. What was I to think of his obese analysis, what of a biography in which the biographer hates his subject from the bottom of his heart and traces anything and everything down to the slightest comma back to

Hemingway's mother complex, no matter whether it dealt with the erotic stimulating role of girls with bobbed haircuts or with the alcoholism in his life.

That's not a biography, I thought to myself, rather a story about a sick man, built on the fact that his mother put the two-year-old in girls' clothes, called him "Summer Girl," and, on top of all that, when he had become older, forced him to play the cello. No one in the world played worse than he did. Besides, the biographical is continually made the surveyor's rod of the written described in his books. Not the stories, rather what the critics and professors knew or believed they knew about the life of the author furnish the basis of his interpretations. Oh, those professors! They owned libraries from which they learned nothing.

Hemingway knew about such problems when he said to Hotchner: *You know the professors in their thin, erudite volumes describe my unhappy childhood which supposedly motivated all my literary drives. . . . [They] feed my collected works into their Symbol Searcher, which is a cross between a Geiger counter and a pinball machine, or maybe they use their economy-sized death-wish indicators, which can also turn up complexes, both certified and uncertified, at the flick of the dial.*

Again and again his mother, called "the bitch" by her

son her whole life, is depicted by Lynn as a larger-than-life, tyrannical manager of the emotional life of her son. That mother, who wanted to be a singer but could not stand the glaring spotlight of Madison Square Garden, while his father had been occupied in front of tall cabinets containing salamanders, snakes, toads, and lizards in alcohol or, better yet, had gone hunting! That mother had given her son the revolver with which his father had killed himself—and packed a chocolate cake with it. Not only had father and son killed themselves, but also his favorite sister, Ursula, and his brother Leicester, as well as his last love, the futilely courted Adriana Ivancich with the Byzantine nose. Has anyone whose parents were normal ever created art?

But a close friend of Hemingway's said once, on the subject of his mother: *I don't believe that he considered the suicide of his father cowardly. For him it was only the natural consequence of the behavior of his mother toward his father. He put the blame for the death on her. That's why he never wrote a novel that takes place in America. He once said to me: I can't do it as long as my mother is still alive, considering what I would have to write about her. Then, when she died, I asked: Do you now want to write your American novel? No, he said, it's too late.*

That kind of thing didn't matter to the lady journalist.

His work is just crawling everywhere with sexual anxieties, she asserted, agreeing with Professor Lynn. Typical American research below the belt where it says: *Taken altogether his attacks showed Hemingway as a jealous, extremely egocentric, and enormously ambitious writer with the provocative behavior of an athlete stepping up for a contest. By above all aiming at sexual susceptibilities, he seemed to want to prove his own invulnerability. And still, doing that, he proved the exact opposite.*

Besides, there was too much pathos involved for me, when Lynn says: *Hemingway's pain began in his childhood and extended to his death like the waves on a quiet lake when one dips his hand in.*

How does that fit in with Lynn's stupendous evidence of Hemingway's fondness for sweets, which is connected to his position in sexual intercourse.

And the lady journalist went one step further when she asserted: "The thing is simply that Hemingway staged his own myth so much bigger than life with the help of the media in the first half of his life (so that he could hide behind it) that in the second half of his life he destroyed himself trying to live up to his legend. When for a long time he no longer knew what the sense of winning is, he found victory in death."

These statements made me uneasy. The lady journalist had succeeded in all seriousness in leaving a few scratches, even wounds, on my image of Hemingway. For this woman Hemingway had not been *a whole man!*

Meanwhile Papa was no longer the hard-boiled camp follower and globetrotter, the hard-drinking woman and lion chaser—*only three things have been fun in my life: hunting, writing, and sleeping with a woman*—the sportsman, the daredevil, Nobel Prize Laureate, world champion of all classes, the bullfight aficionado, and high-seas fisherman, for which I had so admired him. The lady journalist had sundered the whole man with the help of the American professor.

No matter whether he was a braggart or macho: for me he remained *my* Papa. Without *my* Hemingway I felt impoverished. My old childhood fear crept into me and sat like a frog in my throat.

And the journalist had another witness: Gertrude Stein. Even she had recognized what lurked behind the loud brutality of the Kansas City boy: *For Hemingway everything was multiplied by sex and death, or subtracted by them. I knew from the very beginning, and I know now even better, that for him it wasn't merely to get to the heart of things; they were only the mask for the tenderness and goodness in him, and then his torturous shyness fled into brutality.*

In addition, the journalist referred to a letter from Hemingway's mother: "A mother's love seems to me like a bank. Each child that is born to her enters the world with a large and prosperous bank account, seemingly inexhaustible. For the first five years he draws and draws. . . . There are no deposits in the bank account during all the early years. . . . Then, for the next ten years, or so, up to adolescence . . . the bank is heavily drawn upon . . . —there are a few deposits of pennies. . . . Truly, the bank account is perilously low. . . . The bank is still paying out love, sympathy with wrongs, and enthusiasm for all ventures. . . . The account needs some deposits, . . . some good sized ones in the way of gratitude and appreciation. . . . —there is nothing before you but bankruptcy: *You have overdrawn.*"

I advanced in my thoughts against Gertrude Stein what she had said about Hitler, who, in her opinion, should have earned the Nobel Peace Prize: "Hitler will never foment a war," Stein said. I cried out, and I imagined a debate with the journalist. "He is not the dangerous one. He is a German Romanticist. He wants the illusion of victory and power, the glamour and the glory of war, but the blood and the battles that are necessary to win the war he would not have been able to bear. No, Mussolini—he's the dangerous man, because he's an Italian realist. He wouldn't stop at anything."

But the lady journalist had disposed of that, presumably with a smile. I had to give in, and that hurt, for I didn't want to chase along after a phantom for whom lying about his experiences had become second nature, I didn't want to be taken in by a braggart and a brawler—a psychiatric case was of no interest to me. I was interested in the suitcase. The critic, thank God, hadn't the slightest inkling about the suitcase. Never heard of it!

When I was sitting until late at night in the hotel bar and thinking about the newspaper article, a stranger—who was looking for any kind of response and was presumably as alone as I was—told me an entirely different story:

He had a strange love affair behind him. It had involved a woman who taught aerobics to sick people and was a music pedagogue who directed a nursing home. Student nurses had reported that the music teacher had tied her invalids to the bed and beaten them. In addition, medicines covered by anaesthetic regulations were found by the sackful. The local office responsible had already issued penalties against the director of the home because spoiled foodstuffs had been found there. Several old people had testified that they had been tied up, struck on their heads and arms, and pulled by their hair. In three cases the aerobics instructor had taken objects from the effects of patients who had died. Besides, she had tried to charge for overpriced courses of treatment and to continue receiving money for courses of treatment of patients who had already died. And he had loved that woman.

Later, in my dreams, the figure of the critic merged with that of the aerobics instructor, who at the end looked like Gertrude Stein with her Caesar haircut.

19

"Let's go fishing," Berni said in that endless summer way back then. "I know a couple of good spots," he said, when we were sauntering in the direction of the vacation resort.

"We ought to take a girl along," I suggested, because I was in the mood for one, although I had a Hemingway volume in my pocket: *Men without Women*. A yellow paperback with a black bull with white horns on the cover. I had just recently bought it at my bookseller's, the Waterwheel Professor.

"I don't know," said Berni, "girls are mostly a nuisance, and they don't know anything about fishing. Besides, they're repulsed by worms."

"But there are a couple of nice chicks on the way," I retorted and thought of the vacation guests.

Berni drove cautiously into a curve and concentrated on the road like a bus driver. On the back seat his father's fishing gear rattled. It was an asphalt road, not so very wide, on which there was hardly any traffic and which was seldom patrolled by the police. I took a swallow from a Coke bottle and passed it to Berni, who likewise drank. Then we laughed. It was a hot day, and we were sweating from doing nothing. We went past the resort, where people were lying in reclining chairs under umbrellas in the garden. Mostly they were families from the Rhineland who could afford such a thing. As a rule the children were rather little, but once in a while an older married couple was present with girls our age. That news quickly spread among us. We met at the swimming pool or at the ice-cream counter, and sometimes something got going. At least a little bit. Behind the resort began the woods, then came the endless meadows, until again a small stand of woods appeared, through which the river slithered listlessly. "River" is an exaggeration. It was a fairly good-sized brook with pretty cold water, not deep enough for swimming and with too-sharp rocks. As we left the first woods, a girl approached us. She was alone.

"Hey, stop!" I yelled at Berni, who was about to shift into a higher gear.

"Why, what's going on?" he asked.

"Just stop."

Berni drove slower until we were right even with the girl. She was wearing sunglasses, a brightly flowered, light summer dress. We stopped.

"Do you want to come along fishing?" I asked.

She smiled in embarrassment. "Fishing?"

"Yeah, Berni knows a couple of good spots. Trout, you know?"

"I'm not sure," said the girl and stroked her hair out of her face.

"Do come with us," I begged and was annoyed at the soft tone of my voice.

"Let her alone, if she doesn't want to," said Berni and drummed impatiently on the steering wheel.

The girl was silent for a bit and just looked at us.

I got out and bent the seat forward.

"Oh, all right," said the girl and got in. "Why not fishing?" Her voice sounded warm.

We laughed in a silly way and drove on. Berni pulled a sourpuss face. The road became narrower. For a while no one said anything.

"Do you come from the resort?" Berni wanted to know finally.

The girl said yes curtly and looked ahead at the road.

"What's your name?" I asked.

"Corona," said the girl, "and yours?"

"Corona," Berni repeated, a trace too disdainfully. "That's supposed to be a name?"

"Yes," said the girl quietly.

"That's Berni," I said and mentioned my name.

I liked the girl. She had brown legs. Browner than mine.

Berni drove down a field lane, stopped, and unpacked the fishing gear. We sat on the grass and looked at the river. I felt *Men without Women* in my pocket.

"What do your parents do?" asked the girl, looking at me.

"He doesn't have any," Berni said, and spit.

"They were killed in an accident," I added, "I'm an orphan. Live with my grandmother."

"And your parents?" asked Berni.

"Doctors. Is this your car?"

"Sure," said Berni and fumbled with the fishing pole.

"How old are you?" I wanted to know.

"Guess."

"I don't know. Maybe fifteen."

The girl laughed brightly.

"Seventeen," she said proudly. "And you all?"

"Almost eighteen," I said.

I liked her, and for a second I would have liked to touch her.

"And what do you two do when you're not fishing?"

"School," said Berni. "After I graduate I'm going to study medicine."

"And you?"

"I'll keep going to school. I want to graduate. What comes after that I don't know yet."

"Nobody knows," said Berni, grinning. "Whether there even is an afterward," he added.

"I'm a stonecutter."

"Stonecutter?"

"Yeah, tombstones and the like."

"Great," said Corona.

"What's great about that?" I asked and was annoyed at myself at having told her. I seemed like a damned braggart.

We sat there like that and watched Berni, who was getting ready to fish.

"I never went fishing before," said Corona.

"Somehow the thought had occurred to me," Berni

said over his shoulder.

"Is it hard?" the girl wanted to know.

"It's okay," I said, to beat Berni's insolent answer.

"Have you two caught many already? Big fish? And what do you do with them? Fry them or sell them?"

She was asking too many questions all at once. Then she pushed her sunglasses into her hair, and I could finally see her eyes. I liked to look into the eyes of other people. I was less interested, though, in their color than in the little wrinkles around them. Somehow or other I always believed they could tell about the kind of person they belonged to and such. Corona had light-colored eyes and squinted a bit to the left. I again felt *Men without Women* in my pocket.

"I like your dress," I said.

"It's fairly new. I bought it here in this place. Wasn't even so very expensive. I like to wear blue jeans the best. But my mother insists that I wear dresses fairly often."

"Maybe you have problems," said Berni, who was walking down to the river.

Corona put on her sunglasses again.

"Why do you have to have them on?"

"It's too glaring for me."

She pulled the hem of her dress over her knees. Her fingers were long and had red tips. Her fingernails were clean and not chewed off.

Berni looked up at us disgustedly. I knew that he didn't like the girl, or what we were saying either.

"Are you real men?" Corona wanted to know suddenly. "Shall I think that, now, since we're out here?"

"It doesn't matter what you think," I said.

Berni mumbled something to himself. I couldn't understand what he said.

He took his rod down to the riverbank with him. The jelly glass with the white maggots he set down beside him. He fastened the cork float and the hook and waded into the shallow water. The river was clear, and it purled a bit. It was a good spot for trout. We had already been here often, although we knew that we didn't dare get caught. Of course, Berni's father had a fishing license, but that wouldn't help in a doubtful situation. The trout fought stubbornly before you could land them. Berni liked that.

It was three o'clock, and it was so hot that I had no desire to fish. The waiting was irksome to me. Berni had taken off his jacket and unbuttoned his shirt. I was sitting next to the girl, and we stared at the river. Corona was chewing around on a blade of grass. She seemed to me a bit arrogant with her sunglasses. After a while the girl pushed her dress up above her knees and slipped off her shoes. I could see her toes, which were just as tanned as her legs. Her dress was unbuttoned so far that I could look down its front. I turned a little and scooted nearer to get a good look. Corona took a pack of cigarettes out of her shoulder bag, which I hadn't even noticed before. Presumably it contained all kinds of girl stuff. But there was even a cigarette lighter in it. Corona leaned back on her elbows, smoked, and blew the smoke into the summer air. After a few puffs she offered me the pack, and I helped myself.

"Actually, I smoke a pipe," I said.

"And why aren't you smoking a pipe then?"

"Don't have it with me. It's lying around somewhere at home."

"Is your grandmother nice?"

"Nice? What do you mean?"

"I wish I could play the piano. Can you?"

"No."

"Being out here makes me mention that," she said, and blew smoke sideways out of her mouth. For a moment she looked away. I pulled *Men without Women* out of my pocket and put it in my shirt.

"What do you have there?"

"Nothing. It's nothing."

"Show it to me."

"Never mind. It's really nothing."

"Come on, let me see."

"It's nothing for girls."

"Silly guy."

Her sunglasses bothered me. Her legs had fine hairs. That surprised me. Corona looked at me as though she wanted me to say something. But I couldn't think of anything to say.

"Do you sometimes dream that you walk into the river and then you're drowning, even though you're in only knee-deep?"

"Yeah, I do. Sometimes."

"Maybe everybody does," she said.

She stroked her legs with her hand, holding the cigarette in her mouth. Then she reached into the neck of her dress and tugged on the strap of her bra.

We watched Berni. He threw out the hook and led his cork slowly through the river channel. Now and then Berni looked up at us and acted as though he had hooked a fish, and then he paid no attention to us again. I smelled the aroma of the grass and of Corona's skin.

"Do you have a suitcase full of clothes?" I asked.

"Where?" she said, and blew smoke out energetically.

"I don't know. Here or at home."

"I'd like to just take off most of all. Just get away. Anyplace where it's warm and where something's happening. Vacations with parents are boring. I've often thought about it, but every year it's the same."

She looked down at Berni, who had looked up and then turned away again. Sometimes the trout snapped at insects that were so small we couldn't see them.

Men without Women was sticky under my shirt and pricking my skin. Corona stoked her legs again and pulled the dress higher up her brown thighs. They, too, to my astonishment were lightly haired.

"Are you so brown all over?"

"You'd like to know that, wouldn't you?" she laughed. "Actually, my parents are quite nice," she said, "but just a little old-fashioned and boring. My mother's too fat. Supposedly since I was born."

"Do you have brothers or sisters?"

"My sister has already been married for a few years."

"I'm never getting married," I said, and I didn't know why I said that.

"I want to have two children someday. A boy and a girl."

"Would you like to have a husband, too?"

"No, I wouldn't. Don't have to." She flipped the cigarette away. "Were you ever in a bar?"

"Never," I said, "were you?"

"I was allowed in once, though I was still too young."

I stood up and got two colas from the car.

When I returned, the girl had pulled her dress even higher up her thighs. You could almost imagine her panties. I pulled the bill of my Hemingway hat deep over my brow so as not to have to keeping looking at her.

"You didn't want to come with us at all. Why not?"

"I don't even know you two. And I don't know what sort you are. Besides, I think fishing's boring."

"There's nothing special about us."

"How do I know that?"

"Man o man," yelled Berni. His pole was bent over deeply, and the line tossed tautly in the water.

"There he is, I've got him," roared Berni over his shoulder, winding.

"What has he got?" asked the girl.

Corona sat up and watched Berni. He had waded out farther into the water and was holding the pole high while the fish scooted around him.

"Look how excited he is," said Corona, and drank her cola.

I saw the fish flash underwater, then it disappeared

again, and I couldn't make it out anymore. It was a handsome trout, and I knew that Berni wanted to have it for sure so he could show it off.

"The line's going to snap," the girl said.

"No it won't," I said, "you really have no idea. Berni is a good fisherman."

"I don't care," said the girl and lighted a new cigarette. After a while she asked, "Do fish feel pain?"

"I suppose," I said, uncertainly.

"Why is he doing that then?"

"Can't avoid it," I said.

The fish again came up, this time with a white belly. I stood up so I could see everything precisely.

"Come on down and look at this beast," Berni yelled, pulling out the fish.

"It's huge," said Corona.

It was a big trout, which glistened oddly and jerked mightily. We stood around it.

"You don't catch a fish like that every day," said Berni. He was sweating and trembling a little. Then he wanted Corona to get a good look. But she turned away and sat down on the grass again.

"Great," the girl said. "Now catch two more, then we'll each have one."

Berni grinned. "Here," he said and pulled his knife out of his pocket. "Cut it off the hook."

I kneeled in the grass, pressed down the body of the fish, and from below cut with the knife into its gills. The fish made a gurgling sound, and I felt a bit queasy. I thought of Hemingway, to make me feel strong again.

"It's going to taste good," I said, and watched the fish begin to bleed. I stood up and gave Berni back his knife. He wound in the line.

"There's a whole bunch of trout," said Berni. "I'll get them all."

He glanced over his shoulder at Corona, who was watching us. Then he bit his underlip.

"You're going to do it, aren't you?" he whispered.

"Hope so," I said.

He shut his knife against his thigh.

"All kinds of things can happen when you go fishing, huh?" Berni grinned.

"Do you two have secrets?" Corona called, looked at the sky, and shook her head.

"It's nothing," Berni said. "We don't have any secrets. We're friends."

"Well, that's great," she said. "You're all alike. You don't have anything worth hiding."

"I wouldn't be so sure about that," said Berni and scratched himself between his legs. But he turned away to do it.

I went back and sat down close next to Corona on the grass. The book under my shirt was sticking me as though the black bull on the cover were stabbing with its short white horns. Over the water the swallows were chasing insects that had been lured by the afternoon air.

"Do you have a boyfriend?" I wanted to know.

"You mean at home?"

"Yes, I guess."

"No, had one. But that story's over. For a year already. Why do you ask?"

"Just because." I picked around in the grass.

"And you? Do you have a girlfriend?"

"Never did."

Corona didn't say anything. Then she lay flat and stared at the sky. The sun shone on her legs and in the neck of her dress. It seemed to me as though the sun were shining only on the girl. I was protected by the Hemingway cap, under which I was sweating. All in all, I had the feeling of being sticky all over my body. Best of all I would like to have been lying down in the river.

"Fishing you see only half of it," the girl said.

I nodded, for I liked that. There was a remainder that wasn't visible.

"I'd like to go to America," the girl said.

"What do you want to do in America?" I asked.

"Just go there."

She clasped her hands under her head and looked at me through her sunglasses.

"Tell me about yourself," the girl said, "give me a mark of trust."

"I don't know anything about you either," I said and thought about what I could tell her. *Men without Women* I wanted to keep to myself. Then I said: "You know what I'd like to do? I'd like most to build a log cabin in the mountains and have a dog I could go hunting with. And I'd like to have wood under a veranda, and a couple of good books would also have to be there. Then winter could come, and for all I care last half a year. Yes, a log cabin like that, that'd be it."

Berni yelled from the river. His rod bent, and he was holding it with both hands. Then suddenly the rod flipped up high, was straight again, and the line fell flat onto the water's surface.

"Shit!" yelled Berni. "I almost had him."

"Almost, but just almost," said the girl and asked me:

"Would you like to have children someday?" I didn't know what to say to that. We looked at Berni, who was baiting his hook again.

"Oh, well," said the girl, "you won't see me again anyway. Tomorrow we're going home. Then everything will be back to the old routine."

"Are you looking forward to being home?"

"Go on," said the girl, "what do you mean looking forward?"

"Did you ever do anything that you were ashamed of?" I wanted to know.

"Nothing," she said, "nothing that I really had to be ashamed of. I just did it and that's that."

"What did you do?"

"Better not talk about it."

"Why not?" I said. "I'd like to know about it. Are you ashamed of sitting out here with me?"

"Why?" asked the girl. "We haven't done anything yet that we'd have to be ashamed of, have we?"

"It can still happen," I said.

"Your awfully long-winded," the girl said and put her arm around my shoulder. I had nothing against that, although I heard my heart beating. Then I looked down at Berni, who was casting again. The bobber danced on the current. Soon the sun would disappear behind the trees. Then we would drop Corona off at the resort and talk some sort of nonsense about her. And I would bring a trout home with me. My grandmother would be glad and ask me whether I didn't know that fishing without a license was prohibited. And she would wink at me, saying that. Being ashamed was no special feeling for me. You could have a hundred feelings a day. Why not that one, too? In the final analysis, all of that wouldn't be important anymore in the evening, when I finally lay down to read.

The girl took off her sunglasses. With both hands she took my arm, pulled it across to her, and played with its hairs. Then she kissed them. That was strange.

"I'd really like to be happy," said the girl, "my whole life long I'd like to just be happy. I could probably be happy in America, if you know what I mean."

I said nothing, just let it happen.

"Why don't you kiss me?" asked the girl.

I looked down at Berni. He had another fish, but this time didn't yell, just hauled it in.

"He can watch us," said the girl, "I don't mind. It doesn't mean anything." Her face was very close to mine. She opened her mouth and put her tongue in mine. Then she pressed me down onto the grass.

"Kiss me," she said softly, "kiss me as long as you want to."

And I kissed her, put my arms around her and caressed her back and her hips, her face and her hair. I had never before done such a thing, but it came easier for me than I had imagined it so often. My heart was pounding mightily, and I thought I couldn't keep breathing. *Men without Women* was sticking to my skin.

"I like boys," said the girl, "and I wish I could spend the night with you. I like you."

I knew that she didn't really mean that. She just simply said it, but I didn't care. I wanted to say something fantastic to her, but I couldn't get a word out.

"Are you two drunk?" Berni yelled. "You're probably totally drunk."

I lay on my back and had a dry mouth. Corona freed herself and looked down at Berni.

"You're just jealous," she said and looked for the cola bottle.

"I'm fishing down here," Berni yelled, "come on down and see for yourself."

"Let's go," said the girl, but I didn't want to and held tight onto her dress. She freed herself gently and went to Berni and said, "Show me the poor fish."

The trout lay on the grass. The other one, the one I had killed, lay dried out next to it. My fish was bigger. Corona stood silently before them.

"What does a fish like that think, I wonder, when it gets caught?" the girl said and seemed embarrassed.

"Fish don't think," Berni said and fumbled around with his fishing gear. "You can have the fish," Berni said to the girl, "I give it to you. As a souvenir. I don't want it."

"What am I supposed to do with a fish?" The girl looked at the fish, then she turned around and came back up to me.

"You could give it to your parents," I suggested. But the girl just shook her head and sat down again close to me on the grass. She played with her toes. I stared at her brown legs.

"I've had enough," Berni called, and packed his fishing gear together. "You two can do what you want," he said, carrying his stuff to the car. He opened the car door, tossed the fishing stuff onto the back seat, sat down in the driver's seat, and turned on the car radio. We could hear the music. Berni had left the game. Since the car stood some distance farther up, we couldn't see one another. Presumably Berni was smoking now, because he liked to smoke after fishing. The fish still lay below at the riverside on the grass. The girl got up after a while, went down to the fish, picked up some limb or so from the ground, and with it tossed the fish back into the water. Then she came slowly back to me.

"Do you want me to undress?" she asked.

"Yes" I said, terrified. And I thought about how she had kissed me. She unbuttoned her dress and pulled it over her head. In that moment I stuck *Men without Women* back in the seat pocket of my pants. Underneath she was wearing a white bra and white cotton panties. She was brown all over, and the white color contrasted sharply with her skin. Her thighs were strong and her belly fairly flat. I thought that she had looked better with her dress on. I imagined her in a swimming pool, and I imaged a crowd of boys lolling around her. Then she took off the rest. It went pretty fast. I liked her breasts, and I could see how young she was. She turned a bit and took a step back. Then she asked me whether she was pleasing to me. I said nothing, rather just stretched out my arms to her. She came nearer, kneeled down, and pressed herself against me. Her skin felt good, and I liked caressing her. Nothing was to be seen of Berni. Only the radio kept wailing. The girl kissed me all over my face and guided my hands. Apparently she had some experience in these things. But nevertheless I didn't have my heart and soul in it. I can't assert that I didn't feel anything, but the whole time I couldn't stop thinking about my Hemingway collection, and I would much rather have talked to her about that than fumble around on her like that. Somehow I was afraid that the girl Corona would find *Men without Women* on me. I didn't want that.

"What now?" she said. She looked at me seriously. I don't think she expected an answer. Everything was new to me. But I couldn't get rid of the thought of Hemingway. It was simply stronger.

We heard Berni start the car and drive away. He honked twice and made his wheels spin. Corona smiled when I said that we were alone now and would have to go back on foot. But that didn't matter to me at that moment. I had the feeling of having a few things to do. Since we couldn't get enough of one another, we stayed until the sun disappeared. Then we dressed again and started on the way home. We didn't talk very much, rather we walked closely embraced. A good piece away from the resort cottages I kissed her awkwardly and caressed her once more. I still had Hemingway on my mind.

"I'd like to read your thoughts right now," Corona said and slipped away from me.

"I'm thinking of you," I said. That was a straight-out lie, because I was thinking of Hemingway.

"Do you like me?" asked the girl, and smiled.

"Yes," I said, "I like you. And how."

"Do you know now where we're headed?"

"I don't."

The girl was silent for a while. We remained standing. Then she said: "We're still young. But you have to know what's coming. If you don't know what's coming, then you keep running in circles."

I thought about whether I ought to offer the girl a licorice.

"Have you ever read anything by Hemingway?" I asked finally, uncertainly. But hardly had I asked the question than I would rather have ripped out my tongue.

"No," said the girl. "Reading doesn't interest me particularly."

I was very relieved. Papa should belong to me alone! And the bear turd, too.

Grandmother asked whether I had been fishing, but I didn't go into it because I knew that she knew everything without my saying anything. She was quiet and didn't insist on knowing anything about the girl. Grandmother had a sixth sense for everything that I was thinking.

That evening I crawled into bed pretty early and tried to bury myself in the readers' circle. In an illustrated magazine I found the story about how Hemingway had gotten acquainted with Marlene Dietrich. Hemingway told a reporter:

Back in my broke days I was crossing cabin on the Ile, but a pal of mine who was traveling first lent me his reserve tux and smuggled me in for meals. One night we're having dinner in the salon, my pal and I, when there appears at the top of the staircase this unbelievable vision spectacle in white. The Kraut, of course. A long, tight white-beaded gown over that *body; in the area of what is known as the Dramatic Pause, she can give lessons to anybody. So she gives it that Dramatic Pause on the staircase, then slowly slithers down the stairs and across the floor to where Jock Whitney, I think it was, was having a fancy dinner party. Of course, nobody in that dining room has touched food to lips since her entrance. The Kraut gets to the table and all the men hop up and her chair is held at the ready, but she's counting. Twelve. Of course, she apologizes and backs off and says she's sorry but she is very superstitious about being thirteen at anything and with that she turns to go, but I have naturally risen to the occasion and grandly offer to save the party by being the fourteenth. That was how we met.*

I cut out the article and the photos and added them to

my collection in the shoe box. All the while I thought incessantly about Corona and her summer dress.

The next morning I told Grandmother about Hemingway and Marlene Dietrich, but I changed Dietrich's white gown into Corona's summer dress, and I think that I also wove in something or other about fishing and something about brown legs.

"Go on!" said Grandmother. "Those are just stories for the illustrated magazines, so that we can dream."

20

The Finca Vigía, fifteen acres of land on a hill with a view of the village of San Francisco de Paula, lies about ten miles outside of Havana. The taxi driver thought that Don Ernesto had been born twice: once *in the middle of nowhere* in Yankeeland and then for real when he settled down in Cuba. The car drove past the Hatuey brewery, where Papa had celebrated the Nobel Prize with the workers. He had declined an invitation from the dictator, Batista.

The Finca is a milk-white villa and now a public museum, mostly closed for reconstruction. The stucco is crumbling everywhere.

What did I see?

The imposing bullfight poster with Roberto Domingo, deer antlers and a buffalo head that seemed to grow out of the walls, whiskey, gin, Campari, and tequila bottles, a table set, as though the lord of the manor were expected back at any moment, the beloved Mannlich carbine, in a glass case large-caliber bullets very neatly set up in a row, the motor yacht *Pilar* on blocks outside, above all, the weeds in the basin of the swimming pool.

Hemingway loved his Finca, which he acquired for 18,500 Cuban pesos, *because I write better and more comfortably in a fresh morning climate, and because you can stick a piece of paper behind the telephone bell.* He used to write in the bedroom of the house. There was still a special workroom that was set up for him in a quadrangular tower on the southwest corner of the house, but he preferred to work in the bedroom and climbed up to his tower room when *official visitors* drove him up there.

The bedroom was located on the ground floor and adjoined the main living room of the house. The door between the two was propped open by a thick volume that describes *Airplane Motors of the World.* The bedroom was roomy and sunny, since the windows looked to the east and south and let the full light of day fall on the white walls and the yellow-tinted tiles of the floor. The room was divided into two parts by two chest-high bookcases, which protruded into the room at right angles from opposite walls. A wide, low double bed dominated the one half; at its foot oversized house slippers and sport shoes were neatly lined up; at the head end books towered up on both night tables. *I continually read books—as many as I can get. I lay them in opportunely so that I always have a supply.* In the other half stood an imposing, level writing table, a chair on each side, and on the surface of the table lay a stack of bullfighting magazines. Behind, at the end of the room, was a dresser, on the top of which was spread a leopard skin. The other walls were taken up by whitewashed bookcases from which books had tumbled onto the floor. On the topmost shelf of this overfilled bookcase Hemingway had set up a work surface: an area large enough for a typewriter, which was covered by a wooden lectern. As is well known, Hemingway wrote standing up, his feet on a shabby antelope skin, the typewriter and the lectern chest high in front of him. *I wrote the last page thirty-nine times. Until the words took the shortest path.*

What I retained in my memory of the room were first of all the mass of books as well as the remarkable collection of mementos: a giraffe made of wooden beads, a cast-iron turtle, two tiny models of locomotives, a Venetian gondola—*Italy was so damned wonderful. It was sort of like having died and gone to Heaven, a place you'd figured never to see*—a toy bear with a key in its back, a monkey that struck two cymbals, a tin model of a U.S. Navy double-decker, three buffalo horns: *I shot good and thus became a respected local character. It gives me courage again when I look at them.*

But I didn't find the suitcase there, nor the fifty-two cats, the sixteen dogs, nor the three cows—instead of that, a few elderly men in grimy Basque pants. The topic of the day for these men had to do with two monkeys in the zoo that had gotten drunk in the cantina there and had rioted and attacked zoo visitors so that the zoo had to be closed. Up to now there had been no success in capturing the two monkeys. The men exuded the warm vapor of alcohol. The birds sat dazed on branches. In the courtyard stood an old woman, looking at the men and saying nothing. She was wearing a dress worn shiny, with faded little flowers, and had her hair pinned high in a knot. Her eyes were a pale greenish yellow, and it looked as though the sunlight was unpleasant to her. In the quiet one heard the wind blowing through the trees of the inner courtyard, and a hen cackled.

I spent the night in the Hotel Ambos Mundos near the Baroque cathedral, for the *Hotel Ambos was a good place for writing.* Hemingway's room on the northeast top floor was no longer rented out, but visitors were allowed a glance into the musty room, which was darkened by shutters. Next to the made-up bed lay an old edition of *Don Quixote* on the nightstand. "He read in that," the innkeeper said proudly.

In the Bodeguita del Medio, known for short as La B del M, I saw the scribbled walls. I read the names of Salvador Allende, Brigitte Bardot, and Nat King Cole. *For my mojito in the Bodeguita, for my daiquiri in El Floridita.* That sentence hung framed over the bar. I wanted to find out what a *mojito* was. I drank a cocktail called Scarlett O'Hara. Afterward I was drawn into the Floridita, corner of Obispo Street, into the supposed cradle of the daiquiri, where I was offered a cocktail called Rhett Butler.

21

The day after the messed-up staff meeting I had gone to my family doctor, Dr. Theresa Regenscheidt, because of my high blood pressure and because of my suppressed fits of anger that were as unyielding as they were destructive.

"You mustn't repress your anger so much. Out with it! What you urgently need is an extended *vacation for treatment,*" the doctor had said, and for a moment I had hated the young woman whom I otherwise really treasured because of her energetic and frank way.

"*A vacation for treatment?*" I had asked. What was that supposed to mean? It would be the first treatment, the first vacation in my life. Maybe the doctor's suggestion wasn't so bad. But then I had shaken my head indignantly, for I shuddered at the idea of the daily mud packs, and the place that the internist had suggested to me was called Lazybrook Springs.

I didn't want to go to Lazybrook Springs. A few days ago a ten-year-old had been found in the brook. His seventeen-year-old friend told how a quarrel had broken out between the two of them for no reason at all when they had stopped at the brook. In the end the seventeen-year-old had strangled his younger friend and held his head underwater. Without giving his friend a second thought he had then biked home and watched a soccer game on television. The next day he had been noticed by allotment gardeners while he was hanging around the scene of the crime. Already on the previous evening the parents of the ten-year-old had looked for their child and then had reported him missing to the police. In spite of a search that immediately got underway, the child had not been found, even though the mother had located her son's bicycle in a bush near the scene. The corpse of the boy had not been discovered until a few days later. The child was lying in knee-high water, about three hundred yards away from the place where the bicycle had been hidden. Because of man-high bushes and a field of corn, the location is hard to see into.

I didn't want to go to that place. I could in no way recuperate there. But I had to laugh about the story, as I always had to laugh where others couldn't laugh, and vice versa.

"Then, instead of going for a treatment, take a trip," the doctor had advised me as I was leaving, her hand motherly on my shoulder—what familiarity by a woman who could have been my daughter. "Let the wind roar in your face, travel where you always wanted to go. Enjoy your life, my dear. Every day may be your last. Living means planning! But don't carry your preparations to excess, rather consider: All adventures are the result of poor planning."

That thought immediately seemed clear as day to me, for all of a sudden the circumstances of my life seemed to me like provisions that others had taken for me without my participation. Perhaps this was my last chance finally to look for the suitcase. Without having to reflect very long, I had decided on this trip. A bit of misgiving had arisen in me. Would I have any understanding of all that befell me? Colors, smells, gestures, sounds? I felt a deep-seated fear of culmination at the moment of finding Papa's suitcase. I saw myself arrive at my goal and lunge at shadows. Immediately, as medicine against my fear, I acquired a typewriter. Since I could not locate a Corona No. 3 like the one Hemingway had used and called his sole dependable friend and analyst, I gave up on that. I was already looking in my shoe box for the names of the hotels in which Hemingway had stayed and that I had once collected: *Ambos Mundos*, Havana, *Stanley Hotel*, Nairobi . . .

With this decision taken, it seemed to me as though I were traveling with springtime itself. The idea of Hemingway's suitcase had riveted me. Stubbornly I followed it like the fossilized track of an animal that no longer existed on the earth.

"I will find Papa's suitcase," I had asserted to my friend Mürzig, who had wanted to cure me of my mania and as a connoisseur of literature had considered that the search for the suitcase was dubious and wouldn't have even the slightest chance of success. Countless investigators and experts of the Hemingway Exploitation Cartel had tried it long before me, and if the suitcase actually did exist, in Mürzig's opinion, then it would long since have been found and exploited. He was thinking of the Hemingway Room of the John F. Kennedy Library in Boston or the Hemingway Collection of the Harry Ransom Humanities Research Center of the University of Texas. Probably the suitcase had meanwhile been chewed to bits by rats and mice.

I had not let myself be discouraged and had sworn to Mürzig by all that's holy to inform him from my individual stations in each instance by letter or by telephone about the state of things.

Thereupon Mürzig had called me clearly a pathological reading case, but I had countered: At the very beginning of novelistic literature there was a pathological reading case, that is, the reader as hero: The immortal Don Quixote came into being from a mortal named Alonso Quijano through his reading of old tales of knighthood. There were far more important problems, Mürzig had said: For example, the deep abyss between the present and past subjunctive. The subjunctive was more than merely a stumbling stone for grammar. The subjunctive was the synonym for fantasy. Without the subjunctive there were no fiction. Without fiction life were unbearable. Training for the subjunctive was consequently training for survival. That could become, no, that *had* to become an obsession, because otherwise you would have to grab a noose sooner or later. The indicative world was, of course, only a part of the whole, and probably not the most interesting part. For what is real was at best one of the many possibilities of the possible. Behind the subjunctive was the vision of another world that was made visible through language and thus, since it existed only in language, was created by language. The subjunctive! Its German name meant "the coordinator." But for Mürzig it meant "the super-ordinator." It was the real, indeed, the last-possible form of life: the crown of creation. Using it, you could say anything that moved you, and still you had the guarantee of not being able to be committed and not having to commit yourself. The subjunctive was the necessary back door for survival, for if a lesson had to be drawn from life, then it was that one could never be cautious and skeptical enough. The indicative primitive man insulted outright and said: "You asshole." The polite conjunctive user on the other hand said: "I could almost have said, 'You asshole.'" False subjunctive usage would also no longer be considered errors by educated people. Whoever aspired to speak with correct grammar otherwise would reject references to subjunctive errors as hair-splitting or would call upon his so-called subjective sense for language, upon his right to speak according to his lights. It hadn't been that long ago that one believed one had finally gotten hold of the subjunctive. If one had previously been tortured by the misunderstanding of the *consecutio temporum*, in the false assumption that the subjunctive derived from the present tense—today called *subjunctive I* (has, had)—also had to have a function of the present, that the subjunctive derived from the past tense—today called *sub-*

junctive II (had, had)—had to express correspondingly the past tense, then one discovered all of a sudden that this wasn't true. Subjunctive I and subjunctive II both had a completely formed system of tenses and served not to express tenses, rather different degrees of reality.

Having wasn't really the point for me—after all, I had always tried to interrupt the blarney of my friend and instead explain to him my suitcase passion—rather my finding unknown *reading material.* For me the point was the subjunctive of the suitcase, so to speak, for I imagined: what would happen, if . . . I was just nothing more than an *aficionado.* Important were solely the stories in the suitcase. The subjunctive as a modus of possibility was the analogue to poetic invention, storytelling the best means of escaping reality: the indicative. Anyone who told stories or tried to was by nature a subjunctive user. But a subjunctive user wrote no story, rather he read one that someone had written about him.

If an Englishman could travel to Patagonia because of a piece of skin he found in a small cabinet belonging to his grandmother, why then shouldn't a bookseller, who drinks too much whiskey, travel around the world because of a suitcase? Besides, I owed bookselling my nickname *Hemingstein*, which my apprentices in the bookseller academy had given me on the basis of my graying full beard.

Actually, a certain resemblance above all to the photographs of the old and broken writer could not be denied. Even Señora Rodriguez had noticed that. *"Como el americano,"* she had insisted several times, pointing with a smile at the only photograph in my library, in which Papa holds a cat in his hands. I put up with only one other photograph in my library: Arcimbodo's *Librarian*—a man made of books. The works of female authors were strictly separated from those by males. And from the shelves peered the faces of poets.

"Hemingway's suitcase," Mürzig had said, just shaking his head. "Reflect rather on the subjunctive! That would be a worthwhile task: War against all the subjunctive-impaired! The unreal condition is for people like us the substitute for the lost beyond: for Paradise, the anti-world, opium of the people for grammarians. But whom do I mean by 'people like us'? I stand alone and dream of a world in which everyone uses the subjunctive correctly and uses it frequently, doesn't avoid it, has no fear of it. That would be my Heaven. The unreal condition is the open sesame to the second world. The grammarian enters it not like a child ready for astonishment, who lets himself be surprised, but as an initiate. He brings the magic wand with him, a bundle of verbs in subjunctive II; those he pronounces, builds sentences with them, his magic formulas, and it opens up for him. Anyone who has been intoxicated by it can never ever let it go and is immune against all other temptations. The unreal condition drags dreams near enough to touch and at the same time holds them at a distance: They never merge with reality, but a leap is enough, and you're out in the world that exists because you imagine it. The leap is language. There's where you stay back, you poor guys in the indicative, you brave realists, you pygmies standing with both feet solidly on the ground of facts. You see only the abyss in between. It is indeed deep. You fall in through grammatical mistakes. And through timorousness. Instead of rising on the wings of the subjunctive, for what is fantasy other than the subjunctive. The subjunctive opens up to the language of literal possibilities. A subjunctivist demonstrates that he doesn't accept customary opinions without further ado, doesn't accept what is apparently given without testing it. The subjunctivist demonstrates a cautious and distinguished reserve in thinking and speaking. The subjunctivist opens the curtain to the experimental stage. The lover of what is potential lacks the brutal decisiveness of the doer. Just go on and call me intoxicated by the subjunctive. I don't mind that."

But I imagine the suitcase: a not-so-large brown suitcase, probably of leather, with a strong handle, two spring locks and straps for security, already a bit worn out and scratched by the crossing to Europe, a handy thing, just large enough for a pile of manuscripts.

Yes, there would be a few sketches, stories begun, outlines, notes, collections of material and finger exercises, of course, but without doubt the suitcase would contain a few heretofore unknown stories. I was completely convinced of that. Stories such as happen every day, as I imagine them, banal, tragic, and funny. Banality always seemed to be like the suitcase, in which the tragic and the comical are all mixed together. And the result of this confusion was always what was ridiculous. Stories that would otherwise disappear with the suitcase if they weren't told. Nothing grandiose, just simply stories.

22

The fishing village of Cojimar lies about nine miles east of Havana. On the harbor promenade stands a six-columned cupola with a larger-than-life bust of Hemingway, built at the behest of the writer Fernando Campoamor and with the help of the Fishermen's Cooperative, erected in 1962. Papa's gaze is already dulled by erosion. Next to the structure lies the small Hemingway Park: *To the immortal author of "The Old Man and the Sea," dedicated on July 21, 1962. In grateful memory. The people of Cojimar.* The film with Spencer Tracy was made here, and I found out that the extras had received twenty-five pesos for standing around.

Gregorio Fuentes, an old man in his eighties, once the captain of the *Pilar*, reminisced: "Actually, I had known Papa since 1931. Later he took me on as his captain. At eight in the morning we were underway, at daybreak. Often three days in a row. He needed that. To set his thoughts free. For him it was a battle, a sport. Our record was a 1,542-pound blue marlin. Eating the fish wasn't so important. Once on our outings we met an old man and a child, both from Pinar del Rio, who had not caught anything for days. Papa jotted down a few notes. It was that simple. He was always happy and direct. The shot to the head didn't surprise me, however. Papa was in bad shape. I was, too. It was the time of the invasion at the Bay of Pigs by the mercenaries. Papa was good to Cuba."

"What fascinated him about the island?"

"The cool sea breezes in the humid air, the rooster fights, the wall lizards, the punching bag in the sport club of San Francisco de Paula, fishing, naturally." Fidel Castro once said: "Above all, I like the realism in his work. Everything is very convincing, realistic, and there are no shallow parts. And I like his writing about the sea. I liked his courage and his daring. He was an adventurer in the original sense of the word. Namely, a man who suffers from the world and struggles to change it. *For Whom the Bell Tolls* I had already read as a student. You can say that the novel was one of the books that helped me develop battle tactics against the army of Batista. Politically, too, Hemingway was not indifferent to the three great events of this century: the Spanish Civil War, the Second World War, and the Cuban Revolution. Right, he stood up for things, not for ideologies. He was an instinctive man. He knew hostility, even though he was definitely not a revolutionary. But he was a rebel. A loner rebel."

The military attaché Raymond Leddy disparaged Hemingway to the FBI: *The military attaché is convinced of Hemingway's deep hostility toward the FBI. This man will do his best to make trouble for us. We must act prudently to avoid incidents with E. H.* And the FBI dossier continues: *He supports the Castro regime and believes it is the best thing that could have happened to Cuba.*

In the Floridita in Havana I decided I had to drink a daiquiri. Or a Papa Doble, made of two and a half shots of Bacardi White Label rum, the juice of two lemons and half a grapefruit, as well as six drops of maraschino. The ingredients are put into an electric mixer with shaved ice, mixed vigorously, and served foaming in large goblets.

I traveled to Rochester, Minnesota, and circled the Mayo Clinic for several days with a hanging head. The sky was like a low-hanging canopy made of gray muslin, and an impudent wind swept the foliage from the trees as though it were autumn. Evenings in the hotel I, who had eaten my way to a weight of almost two hundred pounds, got drunk. And I got used to drinking whiskey. For, as Papa had said: *You get used to using old Giant Killer and it is able to fix up practically anything. When you work hard all day with your head and know you must work again the next day, what else can change your ideas and make them run on a different plane like whiskey?*

23

The stonecutter, to whom I introduced myself and asked for a position as apprentice during that unending summer when everything began, had arms like a wrestler. He was standing in his apron before a tombstone, had a chisel in his one hand and a hammer in the other. His reddened face with its prominent nose was gray with dust and wet with sweat. I liked it in the workshop, which looked to me quite cluttered. The stonecutter laid his tools aside and looked me over like he would a farm animal. Then he gripped my muscles and made a contemptuous face. It wouldn't have surprised me if he had examined my teeth as well.

"So you want to become a stonecutter," he said and spit. He shook his head. "You're a skinny fellow, but anything can happen. I'll fix that. Do you have good grades? Can you even raise a hammer?"

I begged for the apprenticeship.

The master stonecutter challenged me to punch him. He proffered his immense torso, grinned, and said: "Hit me. It's like steel. I have to know whether there's something to you, or whether you're just a braggart. I won't hit back. Go ahead and hit me."

I punched him, and my fist hurt, while the man laughed shamelessly out loud.

"What would be the worst way for you to die?" he wanted to know, after a pause, jiggling a pencil between his fingers. And while I was thinking about that, he answered his question himself. "The worst thing, my boy, would be getting bored to death." He looked wild. His eyes were wild under his bushy brows, his whole face scarred, that ugly visage, and how he waved his arms. Everything was very wild. He walked back and forth in the workshop, scratched the back of his head, and just left me standing there stupidly.

Finally he said the liberating words: "You can start. Buy yourself an apron and put on decent shoes. Good shoes are important. You need a good stance. And see that you don't come too late. I won't put up with that. I demand absolute punctuality. Otherwise, the fur will fly, and you can just pack it up. Lunch is at ten o'clock. Bring something with you, the work is hard." In farewell he slapped me on the head and grinned again.

When I told Grandmother at home, she gave me good advice: "Don't ever let him see you cry. Such crude guys like it when things get nasty for you and you howl your head off. Don't ever let him see that."

I didn't know whether I was supposed to be afraid or be glad. I didn't know, and I decided to find out.

The first thing I learned was a torrent of invectives and curses. There were mostly curses in the workshop. I was a shitass and a bed wetter, a motherfucker and a stupid pig, a dried-up asshole and a whore's cripple. I was never addressed by my name. I learned to clean up the workshop, sharpen the chisel, clear out the grinding machine, lift the stones, stir the cement, sharpen the pencils. And I was tormented with tricks whenever possible. The two journeymen made everything hard for me, destroyed what I had just finished, spoke disparagingly about me to the master stonecutter, who was made of nothing but fits of rage.

Whereinhellisthatshittyapprenticenow?

Whatdidthatfuckerdothistimethatdirtypig?

Liftthatstoneuphigh.

Cleanuptheplace.

Iwanttobeabletoeatoffthefloor.

Every day in the workshop began by my being sent off with the heavy rubber-tired cart to fetch three cases of beer, because every man who worked there drank almost a case of beer every day. Then came the Steinhäger schnapps that was offered to me, too, until I threw up. They said I had to learn to drink because the work was so dusty and because they had to make a real man out of me. When the journeymen and the master stonecutter were drunk enough, they told dirty jokes, unbuttoned their pants, compared their pricks, and bet a case of beer about which one of them could carry a little plaster cable on his jacked-up prick. They wanted to force me to imitate them, but I declined. Maybe that's why I was slapped so much, too. Not a day went past when the master didn't slap me on the head, punch me in the stomach with his fist, or lay his heavy shoe on my butt. I had bruises all over, but I didn't want to give up. The master stonecutter particularly liked to pinch my ear with his sharp fingernails or pull my hair. "You pissant, how many women have you poked?" That's how it was every day. I prayed to Hemingway: Help me, Papa, help, and I imagined how he came into the workshop and with a couple of left hooks knocked out the master and his journeymen with a crunch. I already saw them lying in the dirt, I was already kicking them in the balls. *I forced him down on his knees and already had my two thumbs good and deep behind his jaw. And I bent the whole thing backward until there was a crack. Don't believe that you can't hear it crack.*

I liked it best when I was sent to the cemetery to clean moss from old tombstones. Then I squatted before the tombstones with the wire brush, read the inscriptions, and set to work. I was alone, didn't get slapped, and could abandon myself to my thoughts while I brushed the stones off until they again shone lusterless in the sun. I was most afraid of carving out the script because with every tap I missed I received a slap on the head. For that reason, too, I was allowed to chisel only the straight lines of the letters. The curves were too complicated for me. I was just too stupid for that, they said. I laid out grave borders, cemented bases, polished stones, and helped lift old tombstones and heave them onto the rubber-tired cart. In the workshop they let me pull the heavy cart all by myself.

Then when I had cleaned up the workshop evenings about six and had trotted home, I was near tears and completely exhausted. At home I washed myself thoroughly, ate supper with my grandmother, and soon got into bed. The

146

shoe box with the articles about Hemingway and the pictures from the illustrated magazines cheered me up again. Besides that I spent more and more time on a short story because my eyes closed with weariness.

My bent back.

The exact placement of the chisel.

The light taps with the mallet.

The wiping off of damp hands.

Here rests in peace.

Tapping script.

Tracing the letters with tracing paper.

The script stencils.

The crackling grease-proof paper.

Just don't spoil the straight lines.

Oh my, you missed it.

Then you can putty it.

Puttying is bungling.

That shithead has bungled it again.

Justwatchityoustupidpig.

Where's the wire brush?

Tracing the inscriptions.

With the fine pencil.

Show me your pencil.

Do you even have one?

Just don't let the ruler slip.

I don't want to see a speck of dust.

Just don't splash any paint.

You fuckingsplasher.

Didn'tcleanupyourpencilagain.

I'll stick your prick in turpentine for you.

Satisfied faces will take you places.

A handicraft as good as gold.

People always die.

A steady business.

Apprentice years aren't master years.

Sayings are truth.

Stupid planer.

Just get out.

Everyone needs a tombstone.

Without a tombstone you've died for nothing.

Why isn't that stone ready yet?

Shutyourdirtytrap.

When I was alone at the cemetery, the wire brush in my hand, the tombstones seemed to me like thick books that I could read. They told me stories about the dead, and they told me of illusion and disappointment. Sometimes I asked my grandmother in the evening about the dead whose stones I had cleaned during the day. But I didn't know anyone dead who rested in peace. Only Hemingway gave me comfort and support. Without Hemingway I could not have survived my stonecutter apprenticeship.

Sometimes I wrote the life stories of the dead in my notebook. I understood that too little was on the tombstones, for what was written large there? Family name and first name, born, died. But what lay between? What the master inscribed in the stones, that was one thing, but what I scraped free with the wire brush, that was something else. The story of the dead did not interest the master, but it kept me busy when I worked alone at the cemetery. For in reality I was not scraping moss and dirt from the tombstones at all, rather I was revealing the stories of the buried and spinning them back to life. What was past could not be squeezed between two dates. But the master and his journeymen had no idea of all that. All that counted for them was what they could write on the bill. Again, nothing but numbers. Satisfied faces will get you places. With the stories of the dead I discovered something that I could keep for myself. I began to write down the stories of the dead like maybe Hemingway did his short stories. The dead taught me about life. I treated every one of them the same: whether drunkard or champion shot. The only things that kept memory alert and made the past not past were the stories of the dead. And

I imagined inscribing the stories secretly onto the tombstones so that they would be preserved and make of the cemetery a place where the stories remained alive because they were told by the tombstones as though by books. All the dead were gathered here, waiting for an eternity that had been promised them with falsehood and deceit.

Bled dry by ambition.

Driven out of my house, tossed to the wind, and a bride in every harbor.

I—an old maid, chaste into my cool grave. But got rich as Croesus and died without heirs.

Worn down by poverty and labor until one day in anger about my life I slew a guy.

I am the gaunt face with the crushed eye.

Life was easy for me, but I had a loose mouth.

He was nice to me, left me with a kid, left me in the lurch, until I went into the lake.

A stall full of kids, and not one is left.

They all died in battle.

How is it that I'm lying here, unnoticed and forgotten, when not a single skirt was safe from me?

I always hammered in little nails and bored thin planks. And that lasted my whole life.

Because I took rat poison I'm lying in unconsecrated

earth.

Until an advanced age I took hikes looking for herbs.

I spent my whole life running gauntlets through blinks, smiles, and winks.

I died an old-fashioned death: of a broken heart.

I repaired bicycle tires for fifty years. Until I ran out of air.

I lost hearth and home playing cards.

Born blind, died deaf. Glory to God on high.

Spent my life smitten by a woman I couldn't have.

Finally dead, once and for all. Why isn't that granted me?

Adornment of the valley, as long as my father was rich.

Such were my short stories, which I wrote neatly with my fountain pen in my notebook. Only my grandmother knew about them, because she had given me information and afterward looked over many of them. The best proof was a shoe box full of pictures of the dead, in which my grandmother liked to rummage. She took out one picture or another, examined the unfocused photo, and told about the life of the dead person. Sometimes, when she was playful, Grandmother mixed the pictures of the dead with playing cards, let me choose one or another, and then spontaneously invented some sort of story for a random name, which didn't always fit. Then I corrected my grandmother. But she waved me away and just laughed.

Sometimes I sat after work at the grave of my parents, picked weeds, watered the flowers, cleaned the moss off the grave enclosure, replaced burned-down candles, or freshened the holy water. And while old women muttered with the dead all around or clattered with watering cans, I told my parents what all I had learned again today in my stone-cutter apprenticeship. Best of all, I read to my father how two row over the lake: *They were seated in the boat, [the boy] in the stern, his father rowing. The sun was coming up over the hills. A bass jumped, making a circle in the water. [The boy] trailed his hand in the water. It felt warm in the sharp chill of the morning.*

In the early morning on the lake, sitting in the stern of the boat with his father rowing, he felt quite sure that he would never die.

24

I knew that the search for Hemingway's suitcase could last for years, but in the end it would be crowned with success. I had no doubt about that. I left out no antiquarian, no archive, no library, no conversation with supposed experts, wherever I traveled.

I looked for the suitcase in Venice in the Gritti Palace Hotel. *Venice [is] the town I left my heart in and haven't been able to find the son of a bitch since,* Papa had written. How can a person live in New York, when there is Venice? I wondered. There Hemingway always played baseball in his room, broke a windowpane, and once after his plane crash in Africa read his obituaries: *Most of them I could not have written better myself. Aside from a few inaccuracies a lot of good was said, which was completely undeserved. Most amusing was to read in some newspapers about my character and the exact circumstances of my death. Some authors demonstrated astonishing powers of imagination. I decided to meet those expectations in the future.*

In Venice I remembered that moment when I had heard the news of Hemingway's death on the radio. Grandmother and I were completely speechless back then, and we sank into one another's arms and cried. Anyway, I remember precisely that I, at least, had stayed in bed a whole day, as though benumbed. I had simply not wanted to believe it.

25

After a few weeks of apprenticeship in stonecutting, the beatings I received daily became too much for me. Crying, I came home and Grandmother said only: "It can't go on like that. Quit." The next day I did not appear in the workshop. I was done in, without work, slapped black and blue, and I didn't know what to do. I had to try something to come to terms with all of that. I had to get moving, and I didn't know what I could do.

Again the readers' circle came to my aid. In a further series about Hemingway the illustrated magazine reported about Papa's friendship with Ezra Pound. Again photographs were included that showed the angular skull of the goateed Pound: the man whom the Americans had locked up in Pisa in a gorilla cage, subsequently charging him with high treason because of his speeches on Mussolini, reprieving him then into an insane asylum, and then letting him move to Europe. Now he was living near Meran on the Brunnenburg. That was a distance that I could go from home on my bicycle. My decision was firm: I had to go to Pound! And for the simple reason that he was Hemingway's friend. And he was so near.

Grandmother laid out her cards, waggled her head thoughtfully, smiled, and let me leave with a hard-cured sausage and a thermos bottle full of tea. I didn't have much in the way of baggage in my saddlebags: a change of underwear, a couple pairs of socks in reserve, as well as some apples and a rain cape, about which there had almost been an argument because I considered it superfluous in high summer. But there were also the *Pisan Cantos*, of which I understood hardly a word, but which I wanted to get autographed, as well as a new paperback by Hemingway: *Paris—A Moveable Feast*.

First, it was leaving Thulsern behind, past the places in the Tirol where wealthy people had located—dentists from the Ruhr or rich Swabians whose grandparents had done their duty for Swabian children before they wandered over the mountains to their misery. I saw lawn sprinklers turning wildly in a circle. The grass in the front yards was kept short laboriously. The sultry south wind constantly in my face, I sometimes looked up at the dramatic clouds, as I had known them from the ceiling paintings in pilgrimage churches at home. I imagined Pound in Pisa and heard in my buzzing head how he began to speak: "They stuck me in a cage made of meshed metal, whose bars had been strengthened just for me. They were for condemned men who were guarded around the clock so they could not commit suicide before they were hanged. Three square yards, ceilinged, a woolen blanket, a pail, concrete floor. Three weeks that wouldn't end. Confinement in isolation. Absolute prohibition against talking. Only Confucius and the Bible. At night harsh spotlights. The curiosity of the other prisoners: That must be a particularly hard guy! Eye inflammation from the dust of the plain of Pisa. And the illumination. The consequence: a tear in the film, delirious states of anxiety, claustrophobia. After two more weeks, transfer to the army hospital. Tents with a field bed and a wooden chest. Strict prohibition against talking. Also meals alone. Handed through the wire. A black soldier, God's messenger, Whiteside, spoke in secret with me and built me a chest. Another one gave me a blanket. The greatest neighborly love takes place among those who don't obey regulations. I managed to get an old broomstick. It became a tennis racket, a battle sword, a billiard cue, a baseball bat, with which I hit small pebbles. I assumed fighting stances, danced shadowboxing, became the talk of the camp. Why is he keeping himself fit?"

The meadows that I pedaled by were for the most part already cut for hay. Here and there I saw children still dragging the heavy rake, while their elders were busy loading up hay or lashing up the hay beam. I met some motorcycle riders coming toward me with high-beam headlights, their leather-clad girlfriends in sidecars. On a high moor stood a sky-blue Mercedes with a lowered top, in which a young man was smoking, his legs hanging over the car door. But for me it was keep on the stupid macadam road that was much too wide, as though it were there to be a landing strip for extraterrestrials. Slowly the headwind lessened, but then I mostly had to push up to the top of the high pass and partly down the pass, too. With the hand brakes pulled until the brake rubber stank, glowing. Innsbruck appeared: the first metropolis of my life, which I had once seen while holding the hand of my grandmother. We came with the rail bus via Reutte, past Martinswand, so we could see the Golden Roof, which admittedly looked disappointingly trashed out. After the city tour, which I hardly remember because there was no lemonade for sale and my hands were sticky as though I had been stirring marmalade, my grandmother had drunk too much red Tirolean wine. In spite of that, she praises it even today. Grandmother's true reason for the outing to Innsbruck was the memorial to Andreas Hofer, whom she worshiped. During the trip there and back she had told about his heroic deeds without pause and thought that a man like him was lacking in the politics of today. It was a shame that the Bavarians at the time had opposed the Tiroleans. Someone like Hofer would show the dirty Prussians the way home today. I couldn't make much of that, since I didn't know any dirty Prussians. Only much later did I understand my grandmother.

I had huge respect for the Brenner Pass because I knew that the name meant hours of shoving through the most awful heat and the hopeless feeling of not getting a step ahead. There were hardly any bicyclists on their way, only once in a while a few farmers with scythes on their shoulders. My desire to visit Ezra Pound seemed to me obviously pretty foolish. Even the place-names irritated me: Mutters, Natters, Matrei. For a while I stood on the pedals and hung in desperation over the handlebars, felt previously unknown acute pains in my calves, while the sweat ran in streams down my back and dripped steadily off my face. Smoking was out of the question. Half the day went past before the customs agent waved me through.

Again Ezra Pound began to speak in my head. His words flowed with the sweat down my back. "The four giants at the four corners are nothing more than watchtowers. In the barbed wire I saw the lines of a musical score. And the birds that flew down upon them in turns wrote me the music. The rain ditches that surrounded my tent were at the same time the dividing lines between the inner and the outer world. I alone was always the silent witness of the events in the camp. I heard the voices of the condemned men, the guards on watch, the soldiers, and the nameless comrades in misfortune. At the first-aid station I later received a typewriter. From September on I worked evenings on my interpretations of Confucius and on the new cantos that I had thought of during the day. The incessant clinking and rattling of the typewriter, which I worked at energetically with my index fingers, was always accompanied by a strum since the platen raced with the clinking."

And while I was sweating over the high pass in the direction of Innsbruck and over the Brenner in the direction of the village of Tirol, I read in my rest pauses what Hemingway had written about Pound:

Ezra . . . was always a good friend. . . . His studio where he lived with his wife, Dorothy, in the rue Notre-Dame-des-Champs was as poor as Gertrude Stein's studio was rich. It had very good light and was heated by a stove and it had paintings by Japanese artists that Ezra knew. . . . Ezra was kinder and more Christian about people than I was. His own writing, when he would hit it right, was so perfect, and he was so sincere in his mistakes and so enamored of his errors, and so kind to people that I always thought of him as a sort of saint. He was also irascible but so perhaps have been many saints. Ezra wanted me to teach him to box. . . . Ezra had not been boxing very long, . . . but it was not very good because he knew how to fence and I was still working to make his left into his boxing hand and move his left foot forward always and bring his right foot up parallel with it. It was just basic moves. I was never able to teach him to throw a left hook and to teach him to shorten his right was something for the future. . . . Ezra was the most generous writer I have ever known and the most disinterested. He helped poets, painters, sculptors and prose writers that he believed in and he would help anyone whether he believed in them or not if they were in trouble. He worried about everyone and in the time when I first knew him he was most worried about T. S. Eliot, who, Ezra told me, had to work in a bank in London and so had insufficient time and bad hours to function as a poet.

To the rhythm of these words I pedaled, in the rhythm of these words I pushed the bike up the mountain, and to the rhythm of these words my determination increased to ask Ezra Pound about Hemingway. My head was in the clouds about the *Paris in the early years when we were very poor and very happy*, with my bicycle headed south on the federal highway loaded with the whizzing aluminum trucks. I had never been so far away from home.

I spent the night in a haystack, full of anxiety that my bicycle could be stolen.

Finally the next morning it was downhill toward the village of Tirol. I asked my way through to Brunnenburg. The people said something about an insane asylum and a crazy man, but that didn't impress me.

My hands hardly felt the grips on the handlebars. I long since no longer glanced at the Tirolean fortified towers or the slowly widening valley. A rhyme, transmitted by my grandmother, hummed in my head:

A fast car came through Mildewiders
And drove through puddles filled with ciders
And in addition to the spiders killed
The stuff on all the riders spilled

The pedal brake stuck more and more, and besides I was afraid the frame would break. Several times the tires had to be pumped up again. I didn't feel too good, and I was more thirsty than hungry. I could have emptied whole village fountains. Grandmother's hard-sausage tips and her solicitous supply of tea were almost used up. Two apples still remained, as well as a little money to spend at a train station newspaper stand. My grandmother called that my travel allowance. A person who wants to discover something, my grandmother had said, must learn to be inventive. Bow-legged, I climbed from the seat. My behind was stinging.

But when I was standing at the gate of Brunnenburg and was about to ring, all my courage left me, and my plan suddenly seemed senseless to me. What would I have talked about with Pound, what could I have asked him? Didn't the old man want finally to be left alone at last? And who was I that I should be allowed to bother the poet?

In my notebook I read a few sentences by Pound, which I had noted down on my way, and I thought all day long about them.

A man understands books only when he has had his share of life. Or in any case no man understands a recondite book until he has experienced or at least come into contact with its contents. The prejudice against book knowledge came from the observation of the stupidity of people who had merely read books.

Reading while the white wing beat of time brushes us, isn't that bliss?

26

I looked for Papa's suitcase in Africa at the foot of Mount Kilimanjaro. Hemingway had loved Africa as though it were a girl: *Nothing can be compared to Africa. Africa and the sea are both the most enchanting whores I know.* It was in Africa where he was happiest in the good times of his life. But instead of the suitcase I found Hemingway's former hunting companions. Most who had been with him on safari were still alive, living in the mountains around the village of Machako, where the Wakamba live: scattered, each with his own family, linked only by common memory. I met the chief skinner, Makau, with whom I became friendly. *Makau was as fast as a trotting horse,* Mary Welsh writes in her memoirs, *he saw a drop of blood or a smeared spoor twenty yards ahead of us.* But now Makau was an old man with a cane, a haggard face already tanned into a mask, with crinkled eyes like a Malay, white hair, and a broken gaze. With stiff fingers the former skinner rummaged in all kinds of papers and brought forth a document and held it proudly under my nose: *Shimoni, Kenya, 1 March 1954. The bearer of this letter, Makau, son of Mutua, has worked on a five-month safari through Kenya and Tanganyika as chief skinner. During this time he prepared with conscientious care the skins of four lions, two leopards, a buffalo, kudu, and impala as well as the usual assortment of other animals and took care especially of ears, paws, etc. He understands his work very well and performs it with skill and proficiency. He is leaving my service only because I will again leave Africa after the conclusion of the hunting safari. I can recommend Makau as an extremely satisfactory, trustworthy, and conscientious skinner. He is also an excellent reader of spoor and would be well suited as a gun bearer. Signed: Ernest Hemingway.*

Also the scout Kyungu had grown old, but his skin was still firm. He told excitedly about King'ee, the man with the beard, about the fire in the camp on the banks of the Salengai River or at the foot of Mount Kilimanjaro, where

King'ee stuck a knife into the ground with its point upward, stuck a hundred-shilling note on it, and challenged his black brothers to take the money: with the mouth and on all fours.

Ngui, the gun bearer, was able to report that King'ee had entrusted to him the secret of writing: *It's just like when you have a hot potato in your mouth. You have to spit it out.* For Ngui the money in King'ee's pockets increased automatically. He often blew his nose into a hundred-shilling note and then threw it away carelessly, sometimes even wiped his ass with it. Ngui grinned in embarrassment. King'ee had already consumed a bottle of gin by eleven o'clock in the morning, then had continued with a mixture of gin and Campari. King'ee had been able to drink without getting drunk, and in the evening he had given boxing lessons in the camps gratis. At night he had driven around in the Landrover through the bush and had shot at rabbits or thrown dozens of shells into the campfire and set off fireworks. King'ee had become envious and furious only when Ngui, instead of him, had been successful in a clean kill, the first shot between the eyes. Then King'ee had been insufferable. And the photograph that Earl Theisen had made of King'ee and the leopard for *Look* had been a counterfeit. Not King'ee but Ngui had brought the leopard down, but had let the man with the beard believe he had been the big hero. Also, sometimes when Masai girls had been visiting, the cots had had to be repaired the next day. Hemingway had even married an eighteen-year-old Wakamba and by doing so, as was the custom, had also inherited her sister, a seventeen-year-old widow. As a trio they had slept on a four-yard-wide goatskin. Hemingway had fathered a son and compensated the family with a herd of goats.

I asked about the son again and again, but everybody simply grinned in embarrassment.

Was it perhaps a fabrication? I knew that Hemingway liked to spin yarns. I found him out with his assertion that he had had an affair with Mata Hari: *One night I fucked her very well, although I found her to be very heavy throughout the hips and to have more desire for what was done for her than what she was giving to the man.* That couldn't be right, because Mata Hari was executed in 1917, while Hemingway didn't arrive on the Italian front until 1918.

And Ngui reported proudly: "In Shimoni we scratched each other's forearms, and each sucked the blood of the other. Then King'ee called me his son and wanted to take me along with him to America. He made it possible for all of us to take a second wife, and if he were still alive and were here, he could make me a millionaire."

On a clear day I took my leave. I hadn't found the suitcase, but to make up for that I had seen how the eyes of the
old men fastened on the snow on Mount Kilimanjaro and in
their hearts heard the familiar voice of Papa: *Jesus Christ!
Shit! Damn it!*

When I reflect on it now, I'm not at all sure whether I
was really in Africa or whether I hadn't found a newspaper
article in my shoe box about "Papa's Black Brothers" and
read it. So vividly that in my imagination I was there and
had talked with those men. It became reality for me,
whichever. I had long since crossed the boundaries that sep-
arate what is read and what is seen, what we so commonly
call reality. And I don't know anyone who could tell me
where the line of separation should run as mercilessly as an
Iron Curtain.

A few days later I met the scout Denis Zaphiro, who
chauffeured me through the region in his cross-country vehi-
cle until he had arrived at a very specific place where he told
me another story.

"On this spot I saw Hemingway in action for the first
time. It was afternoon when he came into my camp. I had
tracked down an injured rhinoceros. It had a broken leg and
didn't stir. Since Hemingway had a hunting license, I
offered him a shot at it. He was very happy. We drove down

the track in the Jeep, then went farther on foot and, after fifteen or twenty yards, discovered where the rhinoceros had crawled. With Koongoo, my spoorman, and Peter, my other scout, we then followed the track, Hemingway on my left. We moved under the shelter of the trees. When we arrived at this tree here, we saw the rhinoceros from the rear. Suddenly he turned and attacked. I said to Hemingway: Look out, it's coming! Ernest raised his rifle. It lasted only seconds, and the rhinoceros was almost upon us. Hemingway fired. The rhinoceros turned in a circle and disappeared in the bush. He was disappointed that it hadn't fallen dead on the spot, and he kept repeating: I hit it, right in the heart. And I said: Don't worry, we'll find it. At this point it turned dark. I broke off the hunt and sent Koongoo back with Peter. They soon reported to me, however, that they had found the rhinoceros. Hemingway was cold-blooded and quiet and knew what he was doing. Anyway, his shot had been perfect. Just think: He was using a .577. He saw early on that writing by itself wasn't enough. Particularly writing about things of which one had no inkling. He was convinced that only dangerous situations could test a man. For that one needed bullfights, big-game hunting, and war."

27

In Nairobi a letter from Assistant Principal Mürzig reached me:

Most esteemed,

dear Hemingstein!

I can only advise you: Drop the matter of the suitcase. It's as senseless as it is hopeless.

Read my story instead.

Yesterday the director had me called right out of class. That's his way of dramatizing and putting himself in the limelight: as though the discussion could not bear a postponement, as though it concerned the life or death of a pupil or a whole class.

It concerned the subjunctive.

I have been told, dear colleague. That's how he begins generally. It has come to my ears. I have learned, that. It's said. It's asserted. You are said.

Yesterday, though, everything pointed to a conciliatory tone. It's been reported to me, my dear colleague. But hardly had he invited me to sit down, with a mellow gesture across his desk, as though he were rehearsing Jesus for Oberammergau, when he suddenly jerked to his feet, placed the backs of his hands onto his butt, but then suppressed this gesture, for he wants to seem perfectly healthy.

They've reported to me, it was parents, concerned parents of pupils in your third-quarter twelfth-year class, and I confirmed it additionally from the entries in your classbook: You've been going through the subjunctive for four months!

I nodded.

Good. You admit it. It's never pleasant for a school principal to have to call a teacher to account, especially when it involves a subject about which the teacher certainly understands more. Your professional specialty without doubt—but four months of subjunctive! I have checked on it, and the lesson plan contains many other important topics, but above all it requires balance—are you listening to me?

I nodded.

A balance between the occupation with language and with literature. It could well be time that you turned to the latter.

I had looked out the window and doing so had the feeling of being years older and having relived this scene in my memory. It had nothing to do with me any longer, I had been fired, the director was a stage figure saying his lines—a familiar text, I myself had written it.

In the evening, at home, it occurred to me what I could have said, should have said, what would have sounded like music to the ears of the director: Four months? Maybe according to the calendar, but just subtract first of all the three-week Christmas vacation, then the flu epidemic in January, where no methodical instruction was possible with the few students remaining. In addition I myself lay in bed for ten days, then comes the postgraduate education conference—there remain, with the other interruptions, the half-week holiday on

Shrove Tuesday, and other holidays, only somewhat more than two months. With three classes of German per week by no means too much for such a comprehensive grammar chapter—

Instead of that, I said: Four months? You're absolutely right! And I'm just getting started with the subjunctive.

Beads of sweat on the brow of the director.

Does that mean you intend to continue discussing the subjunctive?

Intend to? I must.

Mr. Mürzig, I had you summoned to me in the hope of hearing from you that you will now put an end to this subjunctive. It isn't that important either. Instead of that, you say you are just beginning.

Were beginning.

What?

It ought to be: were beginning. Indirect discourse. Substituting the form of subjunctive II for I, because the latter coincides with the indicative. Correctly would have been: You say you were just beginning. If there were still any proof of how necessary it is to take up the subjunctive completely—you would have delivered it yourself with your error just now. For if even a principal makes subjunctive mistakes, how much more so a pupil.

The director made no reply to me. And now something happened that I hadn't counted on: He just left me sitting there. He did not declare the discussion was over, he dispensed with the formula he valued so much, didn't simply send me away, but went himself, and then his secretary came: Mr. Mürzig, I am to inform you that the discussion is over.

Is? Was. You can't drive that devil out in four months.

Now the director communicates with me only in writing.

I used to put great value on the pure separation of the real and the possible and the not-possible and in doing so overlooked where the line of separation runs in truth: not between the real and the possible, but between the possible and the non-possible, both of which one can grasp with the subjunctive. Grammar as a landscape. The blue hills of the possible, the far mist of the perhaps.

Yours as ever,

Mürzig

28

Should I travel on to Fossalta?

I looked at the map. The stretch had to be possible with the bicycle, I thought, while new sentences were already going through my head. Fossalta on the Piave, where Hemingway distributed chocolates and had been wounded by an Austrian grenade launcher, .420 caliber, filled with steel fragments and scrap metal. One of the fragments could have torn off his scrotum. Papa already had the reputation of being invulnerable: *The rep of having one doesn't mean much but having one does! I hope I have one.*

Hemingway wrote home that he was the first American to have been wounded, although he knew that it wasn't so.

First there was talk of 200 grenade fragments, soon it was 227 wounds, then 230 .45-caliber bullets. He claimed to have dragged a wounded Italian an incredible 450 yards.

The place with the memorial tablet would be easy for me to find: *the bend of the river, and where the heavy machine gun post had been, the crater was smoothly grassed. It had been cropped, by sheep or goats, until it looked like a designed depression in a golf course. The river was slow and muddy here, with reeds along the edges, and [he], no one being in sight, squatted low, and [looked] across the river from the bank.*

I decided to turn back. But I chose a new route that dictated *Paris—A Moveable Feast* to me: it led to Schruns into the Hotel Taube. Into Montafon. Why to Schruns? Because Hemingway had written to MacLeish that Schruns was *the* place to read!

A new drudgery began, compared with which the Brenner was child's play. I was so exhausted from pushing uphill in the heat for hours that I fell into a delirium. That went so far that I began to make sense of the life story of Pound from the afterword of the *Pisan Cantos*, which I had bought for a tidy sum from my curious bookseller, the Waterwheel Professor, in order to transcribe them later in my notebook.

On the way to Silvretta—I don't know today exactly where—I had a flat. Red with fury and pale with disappointment in turn, I felt with every turn of the wheel the dull thump of the casing, which slowly pushed over the rim and loosened a bit of tube and looked like the lobe of an internal organ. I jacked up the bike, took off my jacket, spread out the wrenches, the patching kit, pliers, and tools from the saddlebag. While I was sitting there at a loss and had decided to loosen the screws of the back wheel, on my back I felt the whole weight of the Alps through which I had agonized. Then I busied myself with the chain and hated my smeared hands because I knew that the oily dirt would stick for weeks under my fingernails. Now came the lifting out and up, the wrenching of the tube from the casing, looking for the puncture, cramming the valve through the hole in the rim, cleaning the puncture, spreading on the adhesive, blowing it dry, the sweetish smell, pumping up the tube again, yes, now it was holding air, wrenching the casing, the eternal fuss getting the chain on. Finally it was possible to continue on endless serpentines that wound into the fog. But I had again lost more than an hour. The road became more lonely; for a long time I met no one. At a farmstead I found poor lodging and a good soup.

That night I dreamed how Ezra Pound's grandfather

stormed the St. Elizabeth Hospital with Hemingway. Hemingway floored a couple of male nurses and finally the head doctor with his famous left hook, fired a couple of shots from his double-barreled shotgun, riddled the door lock of a barred cage, dragged out the sleep-dazed Pound, clamped the typewriter and a couple of books under his arm, and fled with him. The horse thieves and counterfeiters from among Pound's relatives had taken care of escape vehicles and counterfeit money, which they had weighed out on a gold scales. Pound's father had looted the coinage office that he headed. The poet Yeats brandished his sword wildly and held back the personnel of the clinic. Pound himself delayed the flight again and again with new ideas. First he wanted to present Mussolini with his *Cantos*, and he thought continually about the ceremony, which tie he should wear, whether his shirt should really be black, then again he cursed Churchill, Roosevelt, and Eden: "Bastards, gluttons, equivocators, bled the people all over the country to death. My work a palace ten times the size of Versailles, mirrors that reflect one another, through which the rhymed thoughts are brought forth. Yes, it is a father's house, where there is room for each one of us. The long galleries with endless flights of stairs of a past that hardly anyone else has experienced so vitally, comprehended so thoroughly." Then again, Pound demanded to speak to Stalin and complained verbosely that no one gave him a Georgian dictionary.

Hemingway urged haste, but Pound walked restlessly to and fro in the hospital park and talked without stopping: "'Europe callin', Pound speakin'.' I composed calls for desertion: Every hour that you sacrifice yourself further for this war is lost for you and your children. Every reasonable act on your part means homage to Mussolini and Hitler. They are your leaders. You have let the Jew in. The Jew has rotted your empire, and you yourselves have even out-Jewed the Jews. The expulsion of two million Jews from New York would not be such an exaggeration, if you think what havoc Jewish finance has brought to the Anglo-Saxon race of America. A hundred and fifty radio speeches in the service of the Black Shirts. History registers dirty bastards without respite. When the American troops had taken Rapallo in 1945, I climbed down from Sant' Ambrogio and tried to surrender to a black GI on a bicycle. But he had lost his troop and had something else in mind. A bit later two Italian partisans appeared, searching for fleeing industrialists from Milan. With them I went to Lavagna, a thin-paper edition of Chinese classics in my pocket. I insisted on being taken to the Americans, who issued a warrant for me in all of Italy. I was transported to the headquarters of the CIC in Genoa and interrogated for three weeks by an FBI agent. I repeatedly demanded to speak to Truman and Stalin. If Stalin had granted me only five minutes, I could have shown him the error of his thinking, and we would have been spared all the later misunderstandings and catastrophes. I signed the transcripts of the interrogation and on May 24, 1945, was taken to the military prison compound of Metato near Pisa. It was not a concentration camp but was conceived for the rehabilitation of convicted soldiers, and also as a transit station to many years of imprisonment in the U.S.A. or for the carrying out of death sentences. I was the only civilian, and with my sixty years, the oldest. On the night of November 16 two officers fetched me from the hospital ward to fly with me on the spot to America. I handed over to the guard the book I had been reading and requested him to thank all the personnel of the hospital ward for their kindness. Then I went to the barracks door, turned round, my hands spanned around my neck like a rope, with the trace of a smile, and jerked my chin upward. My son, meanwhile, an American soldier, stood a day too late at the camp gate. What you love ardently is your true inheritance. Veering winds, a floating raft. In a Jeep I traveled to Rome, on a special plane of the air force I flew to Washington, where I arrived on November 18, after two nights without sleep. Chained with handcuffs to two FBI agents, twenty-three dollars in my pocket, the manuscript of the *Pisan Cantos* and the interpretations of Confucius. From the airfield I was taken right to jail. After a night in a common cell I collapsed. Claustrophobia. The American public shouted for the electric chair. High treason. I before the court: a psychological wreck. Psychiatric experts. Mental illness. Could no longer understand. Delivery on December 14 to St. Elizabeth Hospital for the criminally insane. My Elizabethan epoch had its glorious beginning. First in the division for the violently insane. One out of two in a straitjacket. A common room without daylight. Twelve months in that hellhole. In the presence of an armed guard, visits for fifteen minutes. Protests: in vain. After February 1947, transferred: a tiny cell, two-thirds occupied by a bed, and without a door onto the noisy common room, where the television set blubbered in confusion with the senile crazies. Visits in a barred niche. Then from August 1955 in the park. In the summer until eight o'clock at night. In the year 1949, the Bollingen Prize, over a thousand dollars. But it did no good. My case: a cause célèbre in the international press. I: proscribed, spat upon, damned. Dag Hammarskjøld nominates me for the Nobel Prize. Radio Vatican and the Communist Party of Italy simultaneously supported my release. In vain. I was a war criminal.

Old friends came. And again and again: young people. Freaks. Ezra for president, they yelled: Ez for Pres. Sheri Martinelli, painter and ex-model, called me Gramp. Then came Marcella Spann. A young teacher from Texas. My last love. All of America a loony bin."

Finally Hemingway, with Pound in his wake, after a long trip through the forests of Wisconsin on Pound's grandfather's train, reached the liberating harbor and put the refugee on the *Cristoforo Colombo* bound for Italy. The voyage of Columbus: but in the opposite direction. At the end Hemingway recommended that Pound ought to grow sugarcane on the Brunnenburg, and grapes: Ezra's Vineyard! Pound shook his head and said: "It's hard to write a Paradiso when all the outward signs point to an apocalypse." Then Hemingway sent him his Nobel Prize medallion, wrapped in a thousand-dollar bill—after the old Chinese saying that one owns something only when one has given it to someone else and: *because you are our greatest living poet; a small distinction but your own.*

I woke up with a hot head and didn't know what led me to do what I did. Underway alone on my bicycle to Hemingway's hotel in Montafon I had the feeling of having been thrust out somehow into the world, into real life that I had neither known nor really lived up until then. I tried to think of something else, of my age. How old was I anyway? I was young, but at that age one can still have a certain inkling of life. Sometimes I also thought of love and Corona. Then everything came together in me, and something rose up in me that tormented me and cut off my air. Then I was breathing faster without intending to. The world outside was something that didn't even seem to exist right, a vacuum in which I stumbled around without finding something that I could hope to admire, love, and keep, except for Hemingway. Then, when you become older, everything that you did when you were young means nothing at all anymore. I know that now, but I didn't know it at the time. I was just young. Pushing the bicycle on the high pass I remembered having played with a building set as a child. Now it seemed to me as though that could have served only to find out what things were made of or how they could be put together to yield some sort of sense. Pushing the bicycle, I began to understand that I had never taken enough time in all the years to look at anything precisely. It seemed to me as though I had always just flown by everything.

In Schruns, after days of pushing and bleak nights with inquisitive farmers who did not understand me when I told them about Pound and Hemingway, I stopped at the Hotel Taube, where they had a cheap attic room for me. I felt as light as sawdust and on the first evening impatiently had the proprietor show me the guest register. The entry of March 15, 1926, read: *John Dos Passos, Ernest Hemingway, 4 Place de la Concorde, Paris, Hadley R. Hemingway, John Hadley Nicanor Hemingway (Bumby), 2 years, 5 months.* With the party were also Sara and Gerald Murphy, Villa America, Cap d'Antibes, France. The proprietor gave me a photocopy of that page of the guest register. He had no information about a suitcase, and his father had never spoken about it, though he did talk about the last section in *Paris—A Moveable Feast.* In that book everything had been recorded that had happened in his time in Schruns. My bookseller, the Waterwheel Professor, had told me that the work went back to the discovery of two dusty little suitcases in the cellar of the Ritz in late autumn of 1956. Why shouldn't the suitcase that Hadley had missed at the train station also still be found somewhere?

I stayed several days in Schruns, exclusively busy imagining what Hemingway had seen, what he had imagined. *Everything really evil begins with innocence*, he had written. *So you live from day to day and enjoy what you have and don't give it a thought. You lie and hate it, and it destroys you, from day to day it becomes more dangerous, but you live from one day to the other as in war.*

I imagined Hemingway in the large, comfortable room of the Taube, with big stoves, big windows, and big beds. I saw him partaking of the simple meals in the wood-paneled dining room and walking through the broad, spacious valley. I accompanied him to the Lindau and the Wiesbaden cottages, saw him climb with seal climbing skins on his skis and leading the way over the practice slope behind the Taube, while his son Bumby was taken for a walk by a pretty, dark-haired local girl. I accompanied Hemingway skiing on the glacier—*Jesus it was cold. My genital organ to wit penis, pecker, cock or tool froze or damn near froze, and had to be rubbed with snow*—had him drink gentian schnapps, devour jugged hare, and haul red-wine kegs to the Madlen Cottage. I sat at the table when Hemingway played cards with a bankrupt ski school owner from the Rhineland, the local banker, the judge, and the police captain, at their feet a dog named Snout, and I was present when they dug out a dead victim of an avalanche: *his neck was worn through so that the tendons and the bones were visible.* Once a bald-headed German naval officer with dueling scars on his face gave a lecture about the Battle of Skagerrak. I breathed with Hemingway once more the aroma of pines, remembered sleeping in woodsmen's huts on mattresses of beech leaves and the footprints of foxes in the snow. Here Hemingway, whom the local residents called the black, cherry brandy–drinking Christ because of his beard, wrote his first novel. *Finally towards spring there was the great glacier run, smooth and straight, forever straight if our legs could hold it, our ankles locked, we running so low, leaning into the speed, dropping forever and forever in the silent hiss of the crisp powder. It was better than any flying or anything else . . .*

Before my trip home a strange event happened in Schruns. It had to do with a naked woman at a good two-thousand-meter altitude. Over the mountain swept an ice storm in which the forty-year-old piano teacher Gisela Geber went in circles looking for creative intelligence. Later the rescue teams succeeded in recovering the piano teacher's frozen corpse. They knew the woman. Already many times in the past the mountain rescue service had observed how the woman walked unclad in the mountains, meditating for hours in spite of rain, snow, and the cold. Only a few weeks before she had been taken to the hospital with hypothermia, which however did not prevent her from continuing her meditations in the search for "creative intelligence," as she time and again stubbornly called it.

I also spoke with the village tombstone cutter, who complained bitterly about his customers who wanted only marmots and locomotives. In recent times several locomotive engineers had died, all of whom wanted a locomotive as a tombstone. Or a marmot. And he had studied in Florence, Siena, Padua and learned how to carve from stone mourning angels, weeping women, and broken lilies. And now? Marmots, locomotives.

29

I n Berlin I met an old man who had kept dreaming of
one day becoming Hemingway's German publisher. He
had had some success with Dos Passos, but that was
meant to be only the beginning. The crowning achievement
was supposed to be the work of Papa. But it never came to
that. Little by little we got to telling stories, and when I
came out with my search for the suitcase, the old man
smiled. It was an amiable smile, because the idea, the old
man said, could have been his father's.

He had been a strange man and had been well
informed about matters concerning Thulsern. As the son of a
Jewish manufacturer he had pursued various studies in

Bonn, Leipzig, Munich, and Berlin, but he had never managed to conclude any of them properly, rather had temporarily joined all kinds of groups and written unstageable dramas with titles such as *Manometer at 99* and had dreamed of an ideal state in which all races, peoples, and religions would be united in harmony: an impulsive, urgent, powerful genius with the life-style of a Bohemian and the lies of a revolutionary. In Munich he had been sentenced to a year in jail for blasphemy in a poem but had escaped imprisonment by fleeing first to Switzerland, then had withdrawn into Thulsern. There he had spent the happiest time of his life with a wife and children until one day he and his wife had disappeared. They had been taken into custody after a few weeks in Gries, near Bozen, and placed in an insane asylum: the woman at first in Lehen near Salzburg, afterward in Buch near Berlin, where after a ten-year stay she had been released, but had returned voluntarily to the institution and there had died. The traces of the father, however, were lost somewhere in Thulsern. Supposedly he had died in an insane asylum in Valduna in the foothills of the Adel Mountains.

"My brother and I continued the work of our father," the old man said. "Our loveliest time was in Aigen. As a present take my volume *Evergreen: Remarkable Incidents and*

Experiences of a Happy Orphan Boy. And read right in the first part the story of 'The Cottage in the Woods.' Then you, too, will understand why I always wanted to become Hemingway's publisher. Unfortunately, I cannot help you in your search for the suitcase."

I took the book along to the hotel and began to read the story. It praises poverty as an inner glow, takes place in Thulsern, and tells about life in an isolated cottage on a beautiful meadow beside a forest:

It was quite airy: a large room with small windows in thick wooden walls. Through the open door you looked over the pines at the end of the meadow off into the valley. A few steps led to the door, for the cottage, built with its rear to a slope, rested in the center and in front on wooden columns. The roof was laden with large stones. It stood firm against Alpine storms and the weight of snow. But how did my parents manage to hold out in that cottage, which in the winter through February was snowed in? Apparently, they simply didn't know what else to do. Heroism is often nothing more than hopelessness that doesn't lead to ruin.

One night, I remember exactly, my mother woke from sleep with a start, rushed in the dark to my sister's bed to throttle with her bare hands a pine marten that was standing on the child's chest ready to bite through her neck artery.

Instead of taking the valuable pelt, my mother buried the beast under the threshold of the entrance to the cottage, to keep away other blood suckers from attacking sleeping children.

Once my father found the nest of a golden eagle, and the man was successful in bringing home a young eagle. Instead of making money with it, he built it a birdhouse . . .

I understood the old man with his life's dream of becoming Hemingway's publisher, for the story pointed directly at Papa's hero Nick up in Michigan.

30

In Hong Kong, which Hemingway had visited with Martha Gellhorn, I bought myself a jacket that had to look just like Papa's beloved Hong Kong jacket, large-checkered with huge sewed-on pockets, especially safe from pickpockets. In what he called his racing jacket he looked like a pregnant bear. I had to forgo the visit to Shaokwan, Chungking, and Rangoon. That wasn't hard because for inexplicable reasons I did not think the suitcase was there. That corner of the world was important only in connection with the purchase of the jacket.

I put up at a very fine hotel and, when handed hot sauna cloths for my face when checking in, one of those perfect smiling angels asked me whether I was traveling alone. When I naively said yes, a pretty young lady was offered me who would fulfill my every wish. All I had to do was ask. I inspected the girl skeptically. She pleased me extraordinarily. But I had no desires in that regard, and I felt sorry for the girl. So I invited her to sup with me on the second evening and had her tell me her story. She wasn't particularly bounteous. I was surprised only when I asked what her name was. She really did say Corona. I didn't want to believe her at first. I made it clear to her that I wouldn't let her massage me. She let her head droop, but said nothing. I handed her a couple of bills and so made her smile. After the meal she took me to a bar in which very young girls were dancing on the top of the bar. They had almost nothing on and moved their tiny panties very provocatively directly at the eye level of the patrons. You had only to snap your fingers, and one of the girls came along. They were almost just children. My companion smiled seductively, but I didn't want to. She accompanied me to the door of my room. When I once more shook my head definitively, she rose up on tiptoe, kissed me on the cheek, and disappeared without a sound. The next morning I went past the hotel reception desk to go into town. There a young man was offered me. He sat smiling in the lobby and had very white teeth.

In Hong Kong more mail from Mürzig reached me. Without comment and without the usual salutation, he sent me his graduation speech, which I read holding my breath:

"Originally, honored listeners," Assistant Principal Mürzig wrote, or, as the case may be, said, "I planned to give my topic the only form proper to it: a speech entirely in the subjunctive. Anyone who talks about the subjunctive, I thought to myself, would also like to demonstrate right away what the subjunctive is capable of. I had second thoughts, for on the one hand I was afraid that I could be reproached that I had intended a trick, like someone who writes a novel with a single *e*, and on the other hand, I said to myself: Here, today, it is not a matter of bestowing pleasure upon experts and initiates (if there are any, as far as the subjunctive is concerned, which I doubt), which only they would be able to appreciate, rather it is much more—please forgive this martial expression—a matter of entering into battle against the enemy, or rather, the enemies, above all with the two of them: the false subjunctive and the indicative. Naturally, I mean the mistaken use of those moods. I will leave this lectern as a victor or vanquished, but let my defeat not fall upon the matter at hand, for which I battle, rather fall only upon me, who then would not have understood how to convince you.

195

"Let us begin with an example that isn't ten minutes old. Since I was in an adjacent room at the beginning of this festive occasion, my place down there in the hall was empty, and a while ago through the half-opened door I heard two students in the orchestra talking about me. Where is Mürzig, anyway? one asked. Of course, he didn't say Mürzig, rather used a hateful nickname, but you won't expect me to repeat it to you here. The other, and now listen very carefully—the other replied: They say *he wouldn't come today.*

"Did you notice something? Did you catch the mistake? No? But you should have caught it. To be sure, I know from annoying experience: Almost no one hears that the *would come* is wrong. It would be right, though, if the sentence contained a condition: *They say he would come only if he were to receive a personal invitation.* Or a wish: *O, if he would only come!*—whereby I would have formed that wish better in the negative: *O, if he only wouldn't come!*—for when ever did pupils wish that a teacher might come? *Would come* is the form of subjunctive II, which we get from a past tense helping verb: *he came, he would come,* even though it has nothing else to do with that tense. The very incorrect sentence mentioned should have correctly been: *They say he wasn't coming today. Wasn't coming* is formed from the past tense without a helping verb, and has as little to do with the past tense as *wouldn't come* has. In other words: *wasn't coming* and *wouldn't come* express no tense at all. Subjunctive II serves rather to form sentences expressing a wish, conditional sentences, and unreal sentences, whereas subjunctive I serves almost exclusively to form indirect speech. Such indirect speech is used by almost no one today. It is formed incorrectly with subjunctive II: *They say he wouldn't come* instead of *he wasn't coming*, or, even worse, with the pure indicative: *They say he isn't coming today.* There it's an irrefutable fact that Mürzig isn't coming, and the doubt expressed by *they say* is swept under the rug. That no fact was involved you can see by my standing here: So I did come after all.

"Now, of course, you must be considerate of those who have no command of the subjunctive. Why do they mostly make mistakes? For a very simple reason: There is only one verb, the helping word *to be*, that distinguishes the forms of subjunctive I and subjunctive II quite clearly: *I be, you be, he be, we be, you all be, they be*, and *I were, thou wert, he were, we were, you were, they were*—were that true in the case of other verbs also, we would have no more problems with the subjunctive. Still, there are overlappings and confusions in regard to all other verbs.

"Another case should show you where the subjunctive

can lead us and how helplessly we stand there, if we haven't learned how to handle it. After an absence of many months a man enters his apartment. He wants to go to the bathroom. He does, lifts up the lid of the commode, and sees that a spider has spun its web there. Forgive my excursus to that place on a day like today; I'm taking the example from the novel *The Plunge* by Martin Walser. Now let us take the pleasure of putting that event into indirect speech in the past tense. So: The man says, he had come home, had wanted to go to the bathroom, had raised up the lid and seen that in the toilet bowl a spider—now what? Has been spinning? No, then it would be doing that while the man was looking at it. I must emphasize that it spun its web long before, perhaps weeks before, and now is no longer there. What comes now, dear listeners, you will find in no grammar—the subjunctive made me aware of it. In the subjunctive the language has a double perfect tense. While in the indicative we have three past tenses, in the subjunctive there is only one, so for *I was, I have been, I had been* in the subjunctive there is only *I had been*, and in subjunctive II *I would have been*—so you must just express the sequence of tenses differently within the past, which of course must be possible to express. You do it with that double perfect. The man says, he had raised up the lid and had seen that, in the toilet bowl, a spider had spun its web.

"Yes indeed!

"Is there anyone here who seriously believes that the possibilities of the subjunctive are exhausted with that? To show that something supposedly had simultaneously taken place, such as another event, or previously? Oh no. The subjunctive can do much more.

"Only the subjunctive causes me not to be God. No, don't think me a megalomaniac: I, you, all of us would be God, if we could leap over the ditches that open up between subjunctive I and subjunctive II. For who among us does not dream at times of a better world, which he would gladly create, if only he could? But alas, we can only dream, only wish. God—He can. He says: *Let there be!* and this world *is*. We on the other hand, we must be content with a weak *O, if it only were!* Between that *let there be* and that *were* yawns the abyss. We stand on this side, He on that side. And still you must be able to get across. Do you remember *as though*, and *what if*? That's where subjunctive I and subjunctive II touch, are almost interchangeable, since the ditch is filled up, since there is a bridge. Mankind can approach God, the path leads through the mysteries of the subjunctive. What higher goal could there be? Don't you feel that grammar is much nearer to the ultimate question and its answer than all of philosophy and religion?

"I am walking on that path. From here, from the indicative, I will never find it. I must venture into subjunctive II, I must imagine the Beyond, must produce the better world in my head. What would it be like? That's what I ask; I imagine it; it already exists in me. I open myself up, I hasten there, I will hold it tightly, will force it to abide. Perhaps it will abide only for me, at first, but wouldn't even that be enough? The first step, arrived at through language. I stride upward, on the stony path, on which you, alas, I know it, don't want to follow me. But that doesn't keep me back. Don't deceive yourselves, if I only seem to climb downward, down the steps of this podium—"

At this spot Mürzig's speech broke off, and I had serious concerns about the condition of the health of my only friend and confidant. I did know how thin-skinned the assistant principal was in reality. The whole next day and all night long I remained deeply disturbed. Should I call Mürzig up? I tried it many times. In vain. Nobody answered. Presumably Mürzig had as always driven to his tower on Lago Maggiore to recuperate during his summer vacation.

31

Key word: summer vacation. When I returned home to my grandmother, who had been so frightfully worried, I was very tired, but also very happy. I felt like I had gotten something very important over and done with. I washed thoroughly, but the oil residue under my fingernails remained. A bit later I put Grandmother to bed, because she didn't feel particularly well. The old woman undressed deliberately and lay down. I stood next to her and did not know what I could do for her. "My life has somehow become so thin," my grandmother whispered and turned out the bedside table lamp.

"Yes, that's true," I said, and was embarrassed. "I know."

I wanted life to stop. But it kept on going, and my grandmother got old. At that moment I realized how old she was. I felt alone in a wide, wild land, drifting alone and without a destination. I heard the rushing of distant trains that should take me somewhere, I didn't know where. I felt as though I were surrounded by nothing but blackness. Only the stars glimmered.

"Slowly I'm getting ready to die," whispered my grandmother, "and I want you to know that." In the dimness she smiled a smile that I didn't like. Then she closed her eyes and began breathing peacefully. She had fallen asleep, and I slunk into my room. Suddenly I, too, felt old. I got the shoe box with the articles about Hemingway, looked at the pictures for a long time, and sought an answer to what was happening around me.

All the time I had to think about Hemingway's vanished suitcase. I must have gone to sleep doing that. I dreamed that I was riding on my bicycle to Marlene Dietrich in Paris. I was absolutely certain that she had Papa's suitcase. She was the only one who came into question. I already saw myself sitting on the bicycle seat, saw myself arriving in Paris, riding through the Arc de Triomphe like a participant in the Tour de France and turning into the Avenue Montaigne, a bouquet in my hand. The address had been in the illustrated magazine, and I had immediately written it down.

32

The past thrives lushly on the soil of a sleepless night. Again I lost myself reading. I have always done that, when sleep wouldn't come and release me.

If people bring so much courage to this world, the world has to kill them to break them, and so of course it kills them. The world breaks every one and afterward many are strong at the broken places. But those that will not break it kills. It kills the very good and the very gentle and the very brave impartially. If you are none of these you can be sure it will kill you too but there will be no special hurry.

But I stuck to alcohol and to happiness that would never come to me. And so I continued my life in my own role as the searcher for the suitcase.

Hemingway, I reflected, tried in all his stories not only to describe life but to make it really vivid. So that, when you had read something by him, you had really experienced it. You can't achieve that without showing the bad and the ugly as well as the beautiful. For whenever everything is beautiful, you can't believe in it. Things aren't like that. Hemingway did not believe that good literature has to have anything to do with our times. That was of no consequence to him. The good parts of a book, he thought, can be only what a writer has heard by chance; as he once said, they can come from the weave of the huge carpet of literature—therefore from what has been read—that has been woven further through the centuries, or they can also come into being from the ruin of an entire goddamned life—and one is as good as the other. His comment on that: *As we make our hell we certainly should like it. You can't do anything else with hell but endure it.*

33

The savings that I had put aside for my old age were almost completely used up—my mission seemed at an end, but I said not a single word to anyone about my miserable defeat. Not even to my old friend and sole confidant, Mürzig, for I was too ashamed. When finally having arrived home again, I wanted to go to the toilet. I raised the lid and discovered in the bowl an artfully woven spider wed. Obviously, Señora Rodriguez had overlooked it. I decided to inform Mürzig about it. But first I wanted to have myself examined by my family doctor. My trip had been strenuous, and I felt weary and empty.

Dr. Theresa Regenscheidt behaved sternly to me and

was not at all satisfied with my condition. Some treatment was now unavoidable, for my heart and circulation were very affected. Too much uric acid was leading to occasional bouts with gout; the liver coefficients were terrible. Besides I was complaining about rashes, insomnia, and my heart. Dr. Theresa Regenscheidt diagnosed cardiac fibrosis.

Willingly and touched by fate I accepted the cure in Reeky Creek Springs. Suddenly I didn't care about the repulsive name. The doctor, thank goodness, knew nothing about Hemingway, and I kept to myself that my idol also had suffered from high blood pressure, too much uric acid, insomnia, rashes, liver cirrhosis, diabetes, and cardiac fibrosis. Medical doctors used to be better read.

When I was taking leave of Dr. Regenscheidt, she asked me, as I went out the door, whether I knew how my friend Mürzig was getting along. I didn't know, for I had not talked to him since my return.

"Mürzig has become a mental case," the doctor said and made an unambiguous gesture with her hand. "He broke down giving the commencement address. He had to be taken to the Irsee Psychiatric Clinic. Maybe you will visit him sometime. It isn't far from Reeky Creek Springs. Your old friend will certainly be glad."

Mürzig in the nuthouse? I was shaken, decided at once

to visit him before starting my cure, and drove to Irsee, where I met Mürzig in the best of moods taking a walk in the park.

"Nice to see you, old friend," said Mürzig.

We sat down on a park bench: two aging men in the autumn sun chasing their soap bubbles.

"Your pearl, Señora Rodriguez, kept my house going even during your long trip. But she got on my nerves so with her miserable German that I would have preferred to throw her out, since I cared less and less about my house the more I became absorbed in the subjunctive. But something worse happened, the worst possible turn of events: Rodriguez fell in love with me! The more negatively I acted, the more importunate she became. I would have preferred to throttle her when she disturbed me because of some trifle and then uttered her craving for love in such gruesome German that I felt ghastly pangs in my guts and swore each time to myself really to kill that woman one day. I could not long endure that stomping around on my linguistic nerves. The vision of Rodriguez lying in her own blood began to appear before me. A pleasant, contented feeling warmed my stomach, and each time I had to tell myself quickly that I really didn't desire the death of that woman. But I was able all the more to enjoy my wishful thinking. One day I came home and was absorbed again in the subjunctive when Rodriguez became importunate again and threatened that she would throw herself from the window, if I didn't grant her wish at last. Perhaps I only dreamed it, too, for at the time I was again thinking of the resemblance to God that the subjunctive makes possible. You probably didn't know that your pearl, Rodriguez, is a volcano that only steams under a tightly closed lid. And with me, of all people, she had to vent that lid."

I sat there gawking and listened appalled as Mürzig confessed without beating around the bush that he had wanted to test his daring thesis of the resemblance to God. If she really does jump, he had said to himself, then he would see whether he had any sympathy for the cleaning woman. If so, then he had imagined or dreamed how it would be if she were not to land below.

Mürzig continued breathlessly: "So I pretend to myself that she didn't slam against the ground, and by changing *were to slam* to *didn't slam*, I prevent her from slamming; changing subjunctive II to subjunctive I makes reality of wishful thinking. She doesn't slam. But now I fling it open, the window, that is, and then we'll see whether she'll jump out at all."

But still Mürzig had been terrified when Rodriguez had

started off and in fact had thrown herself out, and instantly he had uttered a whole series of godlike commands in subjunctive I: Let her not smash! Let her land softly! Let her return, whole and uninjured!

Mürzig made only a slight pause to take another breath, bored his finger in the next-to-top buttonhole of my jacket, and said softly:

"Hemingstein, now we are God! Don't worry about me. I had them bring me here to Irsee only because I, as you know, in reality come from an unfortunately out-of-print and never-to-be-reissued novel—I could not say, Hemingstein, that I know you from life—and that I hate regular verbs."

His face twitched thoughtfully.

"One reason for that is that many weak verbs are strong and, to make up for that, strong ones are weak. *Stand, sit, lie*—these verbs express a condition, passivity, as well as weakness: *put, set, lay*, however, an action, so something active, strong. It's the same with other double verbs, with *hang*, with *light* and *shake*. *He lighted* is weak and ought to be strong, *he lit* is strong and ought to be weak. But you can't do much about that. It's as preposterous as *it* for a child and *she* for a ship. Take a look at this," said Mürzig with agitation and handed me a ship's photograph that he took out of his pocket, "look at these forms. In the first chapter of my discourse on the subjunctive I have limited myself to battling for the old subjunctive II forms that are dying out, *spake*, above all for the *a* forms, where there are also those with *o*: *he spake* is a thousand times more beautiful than *he spoke*, and anyone who would say *he would speak* instead belongs on the pillory with a giant sign: *Language Bungler*. Now I'm proceeding. I'm starting with being sure in what I say that I no longer use weak verbs in the past tense. That powerless stuff sticks in my throat: *He computed, he rotated, he surrounded, he debated, he converted, he translated, he attended*. Neutral gear, boredom. On the dung heap with it. I'll no longer allow even the two-syllable weak verbs: *He toted, doted, shouted*: why not *he tat, dat, shat*?

"You must know, dear friend: Mürzig is working out strategems.

"*Ask, usk; drag, drug; say, suy; play, pluy; bake, buke; plow, pluw; bid, bod; meet, mot*; the subjunctive forms would then be, *suey, pluey, pluew, moet*. That must just be carried out consistently, then the language will be strong and beautiful again. *Suffer, soffer; graze, gruze; swell, swull; bark, bork*. If the farmer pluew his field, then more graew there, and the cow would rather grueze there. In addition, the dog would boerk. But, my dear friend, Mürzig isn't content with forming analogies. Away with all weak verbs. Mürzig will make them strong. *Tickle, tockle; heat, hoet; spread, sprod. He would tuckle, haet, sproed. Strike, strake, straked; sweat, swot, swotted*, and likewise with *warm, flirt, swipe, scrape*, and so on. *Lock, lok, loek; fight, fught, feght; shut, shoet, shoit.* Or maybe: *prop, prip, prup; need, noad, nud.* The foreign words are especially ugly, and Mürzig will make them native. *Freeze, fruz, friz,* and then *integrate, integrot, integrut.* If anyone would like to annil this innovation, then he would pervort the strength of the language brung to life, and someone like that, thinks Mürzig, I would loek in jail, for he would have wuckened us."

The twitches in his face became more and more severe.

"Just go on looking for your suitcase. I, too, will take a trip. Mürzig will emigrate, my dear friend, and he will found a Subjunctive Republic, a land far over the mountains, still undiscovered, not entered on any map, Mürzig Land. Mürzig will be the absolute monarch there, will populate the land, will educate all the children who grow up there in the new language. Those will be happy children, and their language pure music. Mürzig will write the great Subjunctive Epic there. Not a single sentence in the indicative. Three big chapters: indirect speech, conditionalis, and irrealis. Form and content will finally merge. Grammar as style and even as plot.

"The hero: a subjunctive rebel.

"For the subjunctive aims at the heart of fiction. It is the heart of fiction. Anyone who doesn't love the subjunctive hasn't even the slightest inkling of literature. If I were a believer, I would add to the Decalogue as a summons an eleventh commandment and coda: *Thou shalt moke use of no false subjunctive.*"

Mürzig sighed deeply before he cried out: "What are we to do, dear Hemingstein, if not go on trips in our wishes, in thoughts? What else is left that we want more than to dwell in our own lives and find our own modest places—you in your books with your Hemingway and I in my, yes, in my subjunctive? But you must forgive me now. A new tutoring session is about to begin in which I must instruct the head doctor in the subjunctive. It seems to me that psychiatrists particularly have an enormous amount of catching up to do there."

A white-clad male nurse appeared, a huge fellow, and took Mürzig into his care. He also let himself be led away willingly and didn't even turn around. A curiously gleaming light enveloped him, when he disappeared in his idiot's castle.

I wanted to talk about my friend with the head doctor: Dr. Kudrun Mazzolini—sparse hair, small, chubby, with swollen legs and a pair of glasses on her hairy nose, thick as the ends of bottles.

"Mürzig, you say?" she asked. "Mürzig. Hm. Yes, without doubt an interesting case. Are you a relative? No? Then I can give you no information at all. Sorry. You have to be related. See this photograph?"

She took a framed picture of a young man from her desk and held it under my nose, as though I was just as nearsighted as she.

"Imagine, that's my son. It is! Perhaps you know his face from the newspaper? Although it has been quite a while ago. No? Try to remember! The Beast of Balderschwang? Yes, you see! That's my son. My son. Hm. Yes. An interesting case. Almost like Mürzig. What did my son do? The Beast of Balderschwang? Kidnapped a girl, a sweet young thing, hid her in a cave, near Balderschwang, didn't touch a hair on the girl's head, just looked at her and admired her beauty. All right, she did have to undress before him. But that was all. He touched her only with his eyes. He's enamored of beauty. An artist. He fed her. A whole week. Then the police found him because he had stolen a flask of perfume in a drugstore. Arrest, the press, the Beast of Balderschwang, trial, sentence, institution. I wrote the decision. Recognized at once the artistic core. Beauty, you know? Took him under my wing. The therapy took effect at once. The man wanted only beauty and to be loved. He can't hurt a fly. Because it's a beast. Sensitive, you know, delicate and with a core soft as butter. Later made him a trusty. Arranged a place for him in the garden nursery, then in the carpenter's shop. He has clever, quick hands. Then he discovered painting. Art, you know? Portrait and nude poses. His first exhibition: a huge success. The painting Beast of Balderschwang. Talented. Even the critics had to admit it. Finally, through friendly arbitrators, got him released early. And adopted the young man. Had myself transferred then from Gemüseinsel here to Irsee. There was just too much talk. Didn't want to do that to my child. Now he is my son. He has sold many pictures and built me a cottage. With the labor of his own hands. Maybe we'll get married. I'm only sixty-two. The Beast of Balderschwang. That would cause a lot of talk. But why not? It all depends on the possibility, oh yes, just on the possibility. On the blue path. That I learned from Mürzig, as I have always learned from my patients. But I can't say anything about Mürzig, even if I wanted. Yes, if you were related . . . , but like this: professional discretion. . . . You know . . ."

34

The blue path of the possible.

The words of the doctor, which reminded me of my old bookseller, the Waterwheel Professor, as well as of Mürzig's advice not to give up my search, encouraged me in one last attempt to find the suitcase after all. I gathered up all my courage, put on my Hemingway cap as always, wore a large-checked woodsman's shirt, and drove to Paris to the Avenue Montaigne: to Marlene Dietrich. My last hope!

I was walking up the stairs to the fourth floor. It was an elegant building. I rang, the housekeeper opened the door, the ceremony of greeting was icy, and I felt my pulse racing when I stood opposite the adored, gracious woman.

As soon as the lady opened the doors to the salon it was as though the light of day poured almost violently over her. I offered the flowers with the smooth smile of a swindler, and I felt in my voice the same chord of exaggeration or lie that official documents have. And I looked at a transparent, triangular face, decently made up, the eyebrows plucked narrow, as was the fashion in her youth. The lady's voice was serious, full of bitterness, enjoining irony and distance. The slowness with which she pronounced inconsequential words indicated to the visitor that he was not particularly welcome. She had the smile of a model standing in front of a canvas just begun. Her face dwindled into mysterious shadows, into masks without a body. It seemed to bend down to me from an infinite height, although I towered over the lady by a head. I looked into hard eyes that lacked tenderness, eyes that had become insensitive to the present. In her hands was something horrible, the stiffness of a futile decision. Fine wrinkles lay like knife cuts about her lipsticked mouth. And each movement was a small token of conspiracy. Only once in a while did it seem as though her glances had insufficient strength to hold out to the end. Therefore the old lady set her eyes on empty spaces that seemed to surround the visitor. As I looked at her almost unashamed, I had a sense that it had to do with a vision of timelessness.

The three-room apartment with three windows onto the courtyard resembled a museum of enchanting antiquities and curios. The shelves were stuffed full of books and records, but I did not have enough time to allow details to affect me: the yellowed photographs of Hemingway, Jean Gabin, or Maurice Chevalier; the certificates of the French Foreign Legion; the door plates of theater dressing rooms; notepads with telephone numbers; stacks of newspapers and magazines. An atmosphere of solemn and macabre stagnation prevailed. And yet the apartment also had a touch of the paltry. The neglected carpet was full of burn marks, the white telephone plastered hundredfold with Scotch tape. In the grave gloom of pulled drapes the partly covered furniture became indistinct in a kind of ghostly softness, like white-skinned primeval animals. I saw pictures that I knew from photographs and films, and understood at once how many clichés I carried around with me in my head. And I registered all that with worshipful admiration. I had entered a lost world. The television set stayed on.

Yes, she was an honorable old lady. And when she had offered me a seat and a cup of tea in the midst of all her plush plunder covered with flowered patterns, when she had sent away her secretary, who, as she remarked smugly, had been at her disposal for many years, when finally I had brought forth my entreaty with some circumspection, she began to gush like a waterfall and kept getting off the subject.

"What do you know about me, young man, and what do you want?

"What did you say you are? Bookseller? I like that. In no other profession are there so many eccentrics. Do you also sell memoirs? Too much nonsense about me has been spread around. What's true is that everything that has been written about me is untrue. I'm not interested in talking about my life. My past doesn't interest me. I'm nothing more today than a banal woman. Once long ago a famous poet came, who always had something going with actresses, and he said to me: O, child, my head and your legs. I never was interested in my career. I always loved music, was the best in my class there: Mozart, Bach, Chopin, sonatas, études, waltzes. I also collected lute straps. At the Advanced School for Music in Weimar and with Professor Carl Flesch in Berlin I studied violin. I was even the concert mistress under Giuseppe Becce, the Nestor of film music. An inflammation of the tendon sheath—and it was all over. Later I often went onstage with the singing saw. An actor taught me how to play it. The saw is especially suited for slow and solemn melodies. I also took the saw with me to the film studio and later to the front to entertain troops. I'm a practical person. I'm not interested in the past. What counts for me is the present, what I have to do today, what I have to do tomorrow, but I never looked back, no. Self-discipline is the most useful of all disciplines. I am a practical person, a logical person, yes? There are no dreams. I worked my whole life, and you don't get ahead with dreams, do you? I have no fear of death. You ought to be afraid of life, yes, but certainly not of death. You don't know anything then. It's over. I don't believe that anything comes afterward. Such nonsense, awful, you can't believe that up there they all fly around, there, maybe? It simply doesn't exist. All that comes from the Bible is just to comfort you. You can't tell me that they are all alive there, up there, and that it must be frightfully overcrowded, with all the people flitting around there. When you've been in a war and you've seen how hundreds of thousands of human beings have been killed—they're all fluttering around up there? That's just not possible. Besides, I don't believe in a higher power either, or the higher power is *meshugge*.

"And now you come to me about Hemingway.

"I was a friend of many writers: with Erich Maria Remarque, with Paustovski. . . . In passing I met many wonderful men, like a ship that passes another in the night.

"People do think that with Hemingway I . . . none of

it's true. Never, never. I loved him. And he loved me. And I have all of his letters, and they are all locked up in a safe in a bank in New York. I'm not ready to turn them over to a museum or to a collector. Not that I believe I could take them with me into the Beyond, but I don't want a stranger to misuse them. They belong to me. He wrote them for me, and no one should earn a penny with them. I will do anything to prevent that. He was my 'Rock of Gibraltar'—a nickname that he loved. At the Ritz I used to just go to his room, sit on the edge of the bathtub, and sing something for Papa or, while he was shaving, show him the mother-of-pearl pistols that General Patton gave me. When Hemingway was in Cuba we wrote to one another regularly; he replied to me 'by return post,' as he put it. I called him *Papa* and liked to sign with *Mama*, while he often called me *Daughter*. We talked to one another for hours on the telephone. Without my having to ask, he gave me good advice. He never said I should hang up and no longer bother him. He sent me his manuscripts and once said about me: 'She loves literature and is an intelligent and conscientious critic. If I have written something I find good, and she reads it and tells me that she likes it, then I'm completely happy. Since she knows all about love and knows that it is either there or it isn't, I give more credence to her judgment than to that of professors.

For I believe that, more than anyone else, she understands about love.' An extremely generous judgment, as always with him. I'll never understand why he loved me too 'strongly,' as he put it. He was an anchor, a wise man, the one who made decisions, the best counselor ever, the head of my personal church. The love between him and me—I don't know what you would call it, but it had nothing to do with eroticism, or with . . . with, with sexuality, no, no, no. Not for a moment. Hemingway was . . . I believe, you know, young man, he was beyond the sexual. I believe he didn't worry about that at all.

"It was wonderful how we got acquainted. Do you know the beautiful old song: *I don't know to whom I belong, for I'm just too much for one person alone. . . . Should something so beautiful pleasure just one? The sun and the stars do belong to us all . . .* ? Do you know it, young man? He was proud never to have slept with me, and he said always that we had fallen in love with one another at the wrong time. Our friendship was the source of a lot of gossip and twaddle. I loved him from the first moment. I never stopped loving him. And I say that because the love that Ernest Hemingway and I felt for one another was a very extraordinary love in the world in which we live, pure, absolute. A love that was raised above any doubt, a boundless love, beyond death—even though I know with certainty that that doesn't exist. Anyway, our feelings lasted for many years, when nobody had any hope anymore to achieve any longing, any wish—whereas Hemingway felt only a deep desperation, just as I did, when I thought about him. Do you know the picture of the two of us in front of the post office in Dietrich, Idaho? He never teased me like he teased other women, and he afforded me the extraordinary privilege of being allowed to call him by his first name. People assume that he was a little afraid of me. But what was written about that was all nonsense. How did I survive his death? I have no answer to that. He taught me everything about life. He didn't teach me anything new, but his affirmation confirmed my most secret thoughts, made them true and strong, and gave them the appearance of something new. He loved me with all his immense strength, and I could never do the same for him. Can one ever return such a love at all? I tried—with what strength I have. He knew that. Since we were separated from one another, the telephone and letters represented our only connection. Every day he told me what his blood pressure was—as though that could have been of decisive importance, and I conscientiously wrote down the rates that he transmitted. He could be happier than all of us. And, what's more important, he could show it, too. His gigantic body seemed to shower sparks whose light fell upon us and were reflected in our eyes. His ability to be happy was in astonishing contrast to his apparent hopelessness. But everything that his 'biographers,' or those who pretend to be such, have written about him is nothing more than a pile of 'manure,' as he put it.

"Back then, on the *Ile de France*, I told him the next day, when we met on the sun deck, how I came across his suitcase. While I was telling him, we went to the railing and stood under a lantern. Every great love begins under a lantern. You see, back in the winter of 1922 I was traveling from Paris to Geneva on the same train as Hadley. While I was saying goodbye to friends on the platform the baggage man must have mixed up the compartments, deposited the suitcase in mine, and spread my traveling plaid over it. Anyway, I didn't discover the suitcase until Geneva and didn't know what to do with it. I opened it. There were only manuscripts in it, signed with the name Ernest Hemingway, which of course meant nothing at all to me at the time. Without having read even a single line, I took the suitcase with me and thought that the owner would show up at my place one day."

My heart was racing at these words. I knew it, I had always known it. The suitcase still existed! I was triumphant and eager to see it on the spot. Marlene Dietrich would get right up and fetch the suitcase. Papa's suitcase! But in the next moment all my hope was undone in a trice.

"When Hemingway had heard my story," Dietrich said, "he laughed with all his might, couldn't stop. No one could beam like he could. When he beamed, he shot me into the sky. Hemingway invited me into the bar and told me to keep the suitcase with its contents, which were no longer important to him. He had forgotten the stuff and long since written it off. Gone and forgotten. And he said: 'Krautsnout, you're the best that every climbed into the ring.' Back then I left the suitcase with my mother in Berlin. It was probably destroyed by the bombs."

And the old lady began softly to hum a song, then to warble: *"The happiness of times gone by are all in this small bag . . ."*

Then she said, with trembling voice and tears in her eyes: "I did love that man."

And it was a while before she got control of herself again.

She began to hum again, then to sing: *"The song is over, the melody faded away. Nothing more remains of the music. Only an echo—of love.* I sang that once for Richard Tauber. But that's another story."

With that the waterfall ran dry and my audience was abruptly ended. The arms with the darting hands came to rest. The birdlike strolling through the room came to a standstill. The old lady led me to the door and said in parting, in a low voice:

"One for my Baby and one more for the road."

Her voice came from very far away. I had listened with the same attention with which I had listened as a child in the dark to Grandmother's stories about faraway islands and mysterious ships. And at that moment I had on the one hand the sure feeling that my whole life had been one big mistake; on the other hand I knew absolutely: My big fish must be somewhere.

35

fter my visit to Paris I returned home by train, discouraged and burned out. Maybe I was one of the last visitors she received in her life. A few weeks later she died, and it could be no accident that when the coffin was removed from the apartment the picture of Hemingway was broken. The popular press took up her death. I collected everything with disgust and relegated it to a file: except for a letter that was published in *Paris Match*. I framed it.

Cuba, July 13, 1950

My very dear Marlene,

You write very well, my dear girl, even if it is a sad let-
ter. We are both two great lonely people and ought to under-
stand one another. I've always believed that I understand
you, but I have never asked you a single question, at least I
hope, except to know where you live or to find out your tele-
phone number. But I have missed you longer and more than
anyone else. I never considered you a goddess, nor a whore,
not even a film star. What I miss is quite simply you, as you
are, and more than anything to hear you sing. But it's that
casual uniform in which I prefer you. I was so proud of you
at the Ritz! You resembled a soldier in battle with your walk
and—certainly a little—with your aroma, in the middle of all
that shit, and with the well-cut costume and the raspberries.
Everybody has already told you: but there's nothing more
beautiful than to hold you in my arms. You know that I like
Ingrid, that I am loyal to her, and that she means something
to me, but holding her in my arms, that's as though I held a
cow. What I'm telling you, you know already.   .

Let Rossellini hold her in his arms, but may those
whom you love hold you in their arms. There's nothing in the
world that compares with embracing you. O.K. Being a
world champion. And maybe being hot stuff! Also, never say
anything against yourself or something about the fact that
you're a boche *or any thoughts of that kind. The way you*

see things is in general the noblest. During the war I thought of you, how you were on our side and how splendidly you carried yourself, while your heart and your fantastic nobility, which made you my hero, had commanded you to be in the proximity of your mother and to bear all the destruction that we caused. You can be whatever you wish, and for all I care you can even make movie Westerns in Technicolor, in spite of that you will always remain my heroine. I hope you are getting along fairly well. I beg you, you must know that I will always love you. I forget you sometimes, like I forget that my heart is beating. But it doesn't stop beating. In case you have immense problems or suffer from a great loneliness, will you come here to spend a nice time?

I'll love you, always, and adore you. We are like a team in a six-day bicycle race in Vel d'His or in the old Palais des Sports. We can always depend on one another, one remains true to the other, and we are capable of doing the impossible or the unimaginable if it's necessary. Both of us have staying power and mental strength, and we never lost the poit de vitesse. The difference is only, you're beautiful and I'm ugly.

I love you and press you close to me and I hug you very tightly. I hope that you don't have too many cares and that you sleep well. Kisses.

As for me, I disbelieve the death of Marlene Dietrich. I can no more come to terms with that than with Hemingway's suicide. Presumably a different woman lies in Berlin under the earth. After all, the actress often enough used doubles for dangerous scenes. Yes, that's how it must be. Dietrich isn't dead. That accounts for the inscription on her tombstone, too:

> *Here I stand*
> *at the core*
> *of my days*

The more opinionated I became about that absurd idea, the closer the thought drew near that Hemingway, too, was still alive. Maybe he only tricked the whole world finally to get some peace. Maybe he still published a few stories under another name, maybe he opened up a small shop somewhere in Idaho and sold rifles: Winchester, Mannlicher, Richardson—double-barreled . . .

At my wit's end, crushed and confused, I got to the sanatorium as fast as I could. Since then I spend my sleepless nights here in Reeky Creek Springs. I read, take extended walks, go on excursions in the post bus to the perversely beautiful landscape of the Allgäu, listen to music, preferably Viotti, but talk to no one.

Following an old habit I was drawn recently into a bookshop. The village of Reeky Creek Springs, as was its nature, had none to offer, so I had to go to Füssen. I entered the store and started to look around. The tight shelves were inaccessible, protected by a supradimensionally large store counter: as though the customer were the enemy of the books. The catalogues lay shut up behind a barred partition. I asked about books by Hemingway. I was promptly rebuked by a surly, hard-of-hearing bookseller. "Sniffing around's not allowed," he screeched. "You don't just burst into a restaurant and eat this and that at will from somebody else's plate."

But I was overcome by an unquenchable longing for bear turds, and my memory blazed up.

In my plans is a visit to a certain Julian Spandig, born in Spindelmühle, a deaf-and-dumb writer who got a degree with a dissertation on lip-reading techniques. Without a steady job or professional practice Spandig lives from the royalties of his father, a naval composer. At the time he was said to be working in seclusion in an abandoned sawmill in Mahdtal on an epic called *Nomads-Land*, which was supposed to be published in mirror-writing.

I sleep miserably. Night becomes day for me, and the days disappear in a single, long night. Then I talk to Hemingway, and say:

"Oh, Papa, I always wanted to have your resoluteness and your straightforwardness, your frankness and tart tenderness, your honesty and your strength, yes, even your sentimentality. And your clear gaze. With you, things are always in their place, they are simple and distinct. You could still wonder and with a pencil transform your feelings into sentences that were right and irrefutable: because they were valid for that brief glimpse of truth about which we have forgotten to ask. You counted your words discriminately, and you didn't bother pondering for very long, but acted. It's a matter of the bitterness of winning and the dignity of hopeless losing, along with the burning desire to learn to understand things. That always gave me a good feeling, really gave me security. As long as I could open your books, I could feel myself sheltered. If you were nearby, nothing could happen to me. Then I was almost invincible. Man, Papa, nobody took your place. You're missed."

Once, sometime or other shortly before dawn, when the light was pale and nothing could be heard but the rush of distant trains, I was startled abruptly from my thoughts, alarmed, and fell at once into another dream. But this time there was no rushing. It was the rustle as though by a wind that made a candle sputter and the flame flare up. Suddenly I had realized that you never understand anything quite correctly. The most important things in life can change quite unnoticed and irretrievably. You're not aware of that at first, because you are so enchanted by the randomness of what has happened to you and all that can presumably still happen, that you sit in front of your own life like a rabbit in front of a snake.

Perhaps I actually never did escape my Thulserian corner and never moved from the spot. Maybe everything was only Hemingway's journey through my head. And perhaps I withdrew my whole life long into my shoe box and rummaged around there and merely imagined everything: because once, several times, many times, again and again I *read* from it and doing so created for myself a world that existed only for me and in which I could feel really good. That, too, may have its reasons and its validity.

But one question torments me still incessantly: Have I missed out on my life because I've only read it, or have I lived it all the more intensely than so many others and thereby received more from the world?

Have I read myself into life or read myself out of it?

Or, reading, have I set it in sand?

Is only that person awake who consciously dreams?

And what is waking up like?

Until now I have found no right answer to that. Neither with Mürzig nor with Hemingway.

Recently I dreamed my grandmother into my room. Her part and the curls in her hair were hewn from stone. She had a pile of readers' circle issues under her arm. The old woman sat down on my bed and said softly: "It is the fate of all human beings that, where their preferences are concerned, they willingly deceive themselves to soften the hurt of disappointments that life brings."

Grandmother bent over me, carefully removed the Hemingway cap from my head, kissed me on my forehead, and with her two wrinkled hands touched my face, held it for a moment that lasted a long time before she suddenly turned away and disappeared forever. But that didn't matter to me anymore, because I was already someone who could be in the world alone and dream about his lions.

On December 16, 1992, the following dispatch was found in the press:

Marlene Dietrich's Mania for Collecting

The previously unknown estate of Marlene Dietrich reveals a great mania for collecting. Her estate, consisting of almost 700 suitcases, cartons, and boxes, has now been inspected for the first time in a shed in Almenia in the state of New York in the United States.

In the suitcases were found collected items, from streetcar tickets of the early years in Berlin to her famous swan piece from the days in Hollywood. She had saved about 3,500, in part extremely expensive, articles of clothing, 160 pairs of shoes, about 300,000 telegrams and letters. She did not throw away even Nazi military memorabilia, such as an SA dagger wrapped in its original grease-proof paper. The world-famous star could no more be separated from arm bands that U.S. soldiers had honored her with during visits with troops in the Second World War than she could from false eyelashes, shaving stuff, and sewing boxes.

After the death of her famous mother in Paris her daughter had the entire estate taken from storage in London, Paris, New York, and Los Angeles and gathered together in

*Almenia. There are said to be previously unknown manu-
scripts found in suitcases . . .*

Afterword

There are no old or finished stories, and sometimes an anecdote handed down repeatedly is enough to start one on its way to circle the globe. In the search for Papa's suitcase a few books were helpful to the bookseller Hemingstein. He let himself be led by them, traveled through them. Ernest Hemingway is quoted from the *Gesamtausgabe* [Collected Works] of the Rowohlt Verlag (1989), among which are the *Ausgewählte Briefe* [Selected Letters] (1984). The statements by Marlene Dietrich are for the most part authentic and can be read in her memoir *Ich bin, Gott sei dank, Berlinerin* [I Am, Thank God, a Berliner] (Ullstein Paperback, 1990) as well as in the conversation with Maximilian Schell (*Die Zeit*, 13, 1983, pp. 39–40). Stefan Klein furnishes information about the life today of *Papas schwarzen Brüdern* [Papa's Black Brothers] in the *Süddeutsche Zeitung*, 4, 1985, p. 75. The view that Hemingway was not a whole man is represented by Sigrid Löffler on the occasion of a review of the biography by Kenneth S. Lynn in *Die Zeit*, 10/1989, p. 108. The Cuba episode quotes Wolfgang Stock, *Die besondere Reise*, in *New York, New York*, 4/1985, pp. 60–65. Chapter 14 quotes Paul Raabe in, *Bibliosibirsk oder Mitten in*

Deutschland, Jahre in Wolfenbüttel, Zurich: Arche, 1992. Finally, Assistant Principal Mürzig is an old, familiar companion, about whom my friend Armin Ayren has written in his novel *Buhl oder die Konjunktiv* [Buhl or the Subjunctive] (Wunderlich, 1982), in his stories *Der Baden-Badener Fenstersturz* [The Baden-Baden Defenestration] (Edition Weitbrecht, 1989), as well as in his essay *Über den Konjunktiv* [On the Subjunctive] (Edition Isele, 1992).

Other sources are:

Georges-Albert Astre. *Ernest Hemingway.* Reinbek bei Hamburg: Rowohlt, 1992.

William Carlos Baker. *Ernest Hemingway. Der Schriftsteller und sein Werk* [The Writer and His Work]. Reinbek bei Hamburg: Rowohlt, 1967.

Gunter Blocker. "Ernest Hemingway." In Gunter Blocker, *Die neuen Wirklichkeiten. Linien und Profilen der modernen Literatur* [The New Realism. Trends and Profiles of Modern Literature], pp. 199–205. Munich: Deutsches Taschenbuch Verlag, 1968.

Van Wyck Brooks. "Interview mit Ernest Hemingway." In Van Wyck Brooks, *Wie sie schreiben* [How They Write], pp. 156–81. Munich: Deutsches Taschenbuch Verlag, 1969.

Anthony Burgess. *Ernest Hemingway.* Munich: Heyne, 1987.

Noberto Fuentes. *Ernest Hemingway—Jahre in Cuba* [Years in Cuba]. Hamburg, 1987.

MacDonald Harris. *Hemingway's Koffer* [Hemingway's Suitcase]. Zurich: Benziger, 1991.

A. E. Hotchner. *Papa Hemingway*. Munich: Deutsches Taschenbuch Verlag, 1969.

Kenneth S. Lynn. *Hemingway. Eine Biographie.* Reinbek bei Hamburg: Rowohlt, 1991.

Archibald MacLeish. "His Mirror Was Danger." *Life*, July 14, 1961, pp. 71–72.

Paul Nizon. *Stolz* [Pride]. Frankfurt am Main: Suhrkamp, 1975.

Finally, for support and advice I am grateful to Dietmar Haack, Eva Hesse, the Loquai Gang, as well as to all those who made my travels possible.